MONTANA BRIDE

LINDA BOORMAN

ACCENT BOOKS
Denver, CO 80215

ACCENT BOOKS

A division of Accent Publications, Inc.
12100 West Sixth Avenue
P.O. Box 15337
Denver, Colorado 80215

Library of Congress Catalog Card Number 85-071304

ISBN 0-89636-180-2

Third Printing

Resisting the urge to scream, I begged, "No, no. Please tell me the name of the man who wrote for you to come to Prospect and marry him."

"Oh, him. Hold your taters," Emmylou said agreeably while she poked around in the pocket of her threadbare jacket. She fished out a folded paper. While she flipped it open and spread it out, I held my breath. "I can't make out readin' much, but his name is Miller."

With that devastating piece of news, she handed me a letter that matched the one resting in my handbag—word for word.

MONTANA BRIDE

Chapter 1

Whenever I smell a freshly cut apple I remember that August afternoon in 1894. In my mind's eye, I can still see myself perched on the back steps of my home, the Bishop Place as it was known around the countryside. With a box of Gravenstein apples on one side of me and a sauce pot on the other, I'm sure I appeared to any observer as placid as the bowl of applesauce I was preparing. But still vivid in my memory even now was the inner me which churned like a bottle of hard cider ready to blow its cork.

As I nipped out the cores and bad spots in the apples, my senses were numb to the lavish flower garden which lay just beyond my feet. The drone of the bees and hummingbirds plying their trade among the riotous August blooms barely penetrated my anxious thoughts. *Would the letter come, or would it not?*

My neighbor's child, little Tibby James, yanked me out of my musings as she shot through the gate in our privacy hedge, screeching at the top of her lungs.

"Miss Mercy, Miss Mercy," she gasped as soon as she spied me on the steps. "Rowdy's did it again. He's a-bleedin' something fierce and we're afraid he'll die this time."

Giving my voluminous apron a flip, I allowed myself to be pulled to my feet and dragged through the gate by Tibby's sweaty hand.

A pile of black and brown fur, the victim lay on an old quilt thoughtfully placed in the shade of an elm tree. Tibby's older sister, Sarah, and brother, Buster, hovered over their pet, inspecting the matted hair on one of his hind legs.

Rowdy, the neighborhood nuisance, did not appear in danger of imminent death, but he did have an ugly, oozing gash on his leg. Being somewhat familiar with Rowdy's harum-scarum lifestyle, I suspected his wound had been received from a less-than-heroic deed.

As I stooped for a closer look, my squeamish stomach discouraged my fingers from touching the bloody flesh and sticky hair. But the concerned looks in three pairs of brown eyes overruled my weak stomach and I issued orders before I could change my mind.

"Sarah, you find a pair of scissors so we can clip all this matted hair away. Buster, see if you can find a clean cloth for a bandage and some kind of healing salve to keep the wound from putrifying. Tibby, you'll have to hold Rowdy's head. If he bites me, you're apt to lose a nurse."

Sarah told me the scissors were her mother's

sewing shears and I suspected the white muslin Buster handed me came from a good bed sheet. But I knew Mrs. James kept a relaxed household and wasn't likely to complain too loudly.

A widow, she worked out by day to support her children. After scrubbing and polishing other people's houses all day, I felt she was entitled to put her swollen feet up in the evening. Father had not shared my compassionate attitude. Forgetting how difficult life can be for a woman alone, he had written the family off as shiftless and the James' home as a blight on Bishop Lane.

Brought back to the present, I realized, fortunately, that Rowdy wasn't the complaining type. As soon as Tibby unclasped his neck he pushed himself upright, sniffed at the lumpy white bandage wrapped around his leg and planted a slobbery kiss on my cheek. This brought howls of laughter from my relieved friends and a yelp from me.

"Eeek! Go away, Rowdy. And from now on, act like a gentleman!"

Tibby dropped to the quilt and buried her head in my middle while I scrubbed at my wet cheek with a lavender-scented handkerchief from my apron pocket.

"Oh, thank you for saving Rowdy for us," she gushed.

I squeezed the soft little body and momentarily laid my face on her sun-soaked hair.

Evidently Buster, who had stopped hugging women two years earlier, had decided the demonstrations of affection had progressed far enough. He grabbed my free hand and began to pull me to my feet. But I sensed his steady brown eyes thanking me as he planted his feet on the ground and allowed me to use him as a prop while gaining my balance.

Before my lame leg accepted its duty, ten-year-old Sarah, who was already nearly my height, slipped her arm around my waist.

"Mercy, I honestly don't know what we-uns would do without you. I know it's not fair to you, but I'm glad you're still living next door and not married to some fellow."

I hesitated. Twenty-three and not yet married . . . . All my troubles came washing back over me. What a relief it would be to share my secret with this mature young girl. But before I could decide, Tibby innocently shrilled, "I heard Ma telling Mrs. Bailey that Lawyer Swindley has soft-soaped Flora into marrying him so's he can get his greedy hands on all the Bishop property."

Sarah snatched her hand from my waist and flared out at her little sister. "Tibby James, you hold your tongue and stop spreading gossip. Did you forget that Mercy's a Bishop?"

Lower lip protruding defiantly, Tibby said, "I don't care. I hate him! Last time he came calling next door, he kicked Rowdy when he jumped on his worsted trousers. Kicked him hard, too!"

"He'd better not let me catch him kicking Rowdy," Buster warned grimly as he demonstrated with his clenched fist the blow he'd give Lawyer Swindley.

I picked at the dog hairs sticking to my apron front and decided I couldn't shift my secret burden to the shoulders of my young neighbor. It was embarrassing enough that Mrs. James, who had a nose for sniffing out gossip, knew about Flora and Elmer Swindley.

I departed hastily and, after a good scrub with

Aunt Dolly's lye soap, I resumed my apple coring task. I'd only tossed two or three apples into the big iron pot when Flora ambled out onto the porch.

I pointedly ignored her. I didn't need to turn around to recognize my brother's widow. No one else slammed a Bishop door or scattered crumbs over imported carpets.

"Hey, Mercy, the postman brought you a letter," she mumbled around a mouthful of chocolate cake.

I froze. I heard my knife clatter as it fell through nerveless fingers to the porch floor. My heart fluttered erratically as if to compensate for my paralyzed exterior.

"Must be from that uncle of yours 'cause it says here, 'Prospect, Montana,' close as I can make out."

Using the porch pillar to pull myself upright, I whirled about as quickly as my crippled leg would allow. On unsteady legs I lurched forward and snatched the letter from my sister-in-law's hand.

Flora, who'd been squinting at the writing on the envelope, reacted to my sudden motions by choking on a huge mound of cake.

Ignoring her hacking, I sped as quickly as my crippled leg would allow down the expansive hall dissecting the house to the front stairs. Grabbing the curved railing, I helped myself up the broad steps to the upper floor, then down the hall to the privacy of my bedroom.

Once there, I closed the door and slumped against it to catch my breath. Even in my anxiety, I allowed myself the luxury of savoring the fact that I'd outwitted Flora. A letter from my Uncle Abe, indeed! This letter, please God, was from a "Christian gentleman rancher desiring a wife." A prince in shining armor who'd appeared to rescue me from the horrible mess brought on by Flora's foolishness.

Although my heart was still racing, I forced myself to fall into the chair at my writing desk and neatly slit the envelope with a letter opener.

Large, bold writing covered the front side of the single sheet of paper.

August 1, 1894
Prospect, Montana

Dear Miss Mercy Bishop,

My heart is overwhelmed by your desire to become my beloved wife. I anxiously await your arrival in the thriving city of Prospect.

The most convenient mode of transportation is the Northern Pacific Railway. Please advise me as to your arrival time so I may ride in from my prosperous ranch and meet your train.

Your Impatient Bridegroom,
Levi Miller

I hugged the letter to my breast and breathed a prayer of thanks to God. The verse of Scripture that read, "All things work together for good to them that love God," must even include Flora's magazine, *Forbidden Love*, I decided.

Soon after Flora had come to live in the Bishop place as my brother Joe's wife, Father had ordered all of Flora's love novels and magazines banned. However, after Father's fatal accident with the runaway horse at the Bishop Lumberyard, Flora had retrieved them from beneath her bed and read them openly. And since Joe's death six months ago, she seemed to have constantly had her nose in one of them.

One day while I was seated at the piano thumbing through music books in preparation for my students' lessons, Flora interrupted me.

"Hey, Mercy! Here's a letter you might like to hear."

I glanced toward the sofa where she sprawled, her snub nose and round pink cheeks hidden behind a magazine entitled, *Forbidden Love*.

Wrinkling my nose, I said rather haughtily, "I really doubt I'd be interested in anything that magazine has to offer."

She shrugged. "Well suit yourself . . . but there's a letter in the 'Lonely Hearts' column from a gent in Montana. Don't you have an uncle out there?"

"Yes, my mother had a brother who moved out there, but I haven't heard from him in years and I can't think he'd be corresponding with a lonely hearts column, whatever that might be."

"It's letters from anybody who can't find a husband or wife. They write a letter that says so and the magazine prints them."

"Oh," I said, curious in spite of myself. What kind of person would write to that sort of magazine seeking a mate? A pretty desperate one, I imagined.

But my curiosity got the better of me. A few

minutes later, when Flora discarded the magazine in favor of the icebox, I surreptitiously picked it up, found the letter and ripped it from the page. Later, in the privacy of my room, I read: "*A Christian gentleman rancher desires a God-fearing wife. All interested ladies send descriptions to Levi Miller, Prospect, Montana.*"

Two days later, I saw Elmer Swindley escort Flora home. I was in the act of raising my window when I witnessed a scene which nearly caused me to tumble through the screen. Flora made quite a sight in her black mourning dress, giggling and cavorting up the long front walk with Elmer practically plastered to her side. My throat tightened in disapproval. With Joe gone just a couple of months, too...

Later, at luncheon, Flora's chatter enlightened me to an uncomfortable degree.

"Mercy, you'll never guess who I bumped into outside Cross's Drug Store."

"I might be able to."

Oblivious to my comment, Flora rushed on. "It was that lawyer, Elmer Swindley. He's so charming, Mercy! I've never in all my days met anyone with such a way about him. He talks like a story."

I stiffened. "Oh, Flora, you know what Father always said about Lawyer Swindley. He's a snake in the grass."

Flora bounced to the edge of her chair and waved her soup spoon in my face. "Mercy Bishop, I'm sick of all of you! You're... you're just jealous—and so was your father! He always thought he was so high-and-mighty. He couldn't stand nobody else makin' money but him. And Joe—what fun was he! I thought when I married on this side of the tracks

14

my life'd started. Was I ever the numbskull...."

Controlling my anger, I tried to reason, "But Flora, Father wasn't the only one who thought Elmer Swindley less than honest."

Flora's fleshy mouth stretched into a grim line. "Well, he's the first man that ever made me feel like a woman—if you know what I mean. And I'm a-telling you, I'm a-goin' for a ride with him tomorrow. And . . . and I'm not a-goin' looking like an old black crow, neither. I'm a-goin' to wear my pink sprigged dimity." With that warning, she flounced away from the table.

The buggy ride was just the beginning. Not one day passed without Elmer ringing the doorbell with an offering to lay at the feet of the "loveliest lady in town." So many candy boxes piled up on the front hall table that Flora satiated herself with choosing only the creams.

Elmer's thin-as-a-coffin body would slip through our oak-paneled front door and wander a little further through the house each visit. By the third week, I was convinced only my bedroom had escaped the scrutiny of those close-set, bulging eyes.

I grew increasingly uneasy. Was it possible that Flora would really marry Lawyer Swindley? An even worse thought tormented me. Would they live in the Bishop Place? Before I could arrange my thoughts into any kind of plan to prevent this, I received a summons from Father's lawyer.

Lawyer Barnes practiced in a tiny office tucked between the barber shop and meat market on Oak Grove's First Street. When I let myself into the hot, airless cubicle, I longed to leave the door ajar. But Lawyer Barnes, who reminded me of a sober Saint

Nicholas, greeted me with, "Close the door, Mercy, and be seated."

I obeyed, then smiled at my friend across his jumbled desk.

The lawyer cleared his throat. "Mercy, I'm not going to beat around the bush. Shelby over at the bank and I are concerned. As your father's closest legal advisors, we feel responsible for you."

My black bombazine dress stuck to my spine. I attempted to stir the air by flapping my gloves in front of my nose. "That's very kind of you."

"Yes . . . er . . . the fact of the matter is, you've been left in a most precarious position. Your father's greatest aim in life was to provide well for his family. He amassed a sizable fortune before his untimely death last year. After your mother's death eighteen years ago he made a will leaving his entire estate to your brother with the provision that he care for you as long as you were, uh, in your single state. In addition, according to that will you were to receive a substantial sum should you marry."

He rumbled to a stop, shuffled through some papers, then peered over his glasses. "Are you following all this, Mercy?" he asked.

"Please continue," I begged.

"Ahem, er, yes. After your father's death last summer your brother took the proper action and made a new will . . . leaving the entire estate to his wife, Flora."

My eyes widened as a sudden, terrible premonition struck me.

Lawyer Barnes tapped a sheaf of papers with a stubby finger and continued. "I encouraged him to make provision for you in the event of his death, but he felt that as you were both young, he'd care for you as your father had outlined in his will. Of course, he never guessed that in less than a year the Grim Reaper would appear in the guise of pneumonia."

The dreadful premonition had become a horrible reality.

The room tilted and my gloves fell from my hand as I clutched the edge of my chair. After a deep gulp my surroundings righted themselves and I found my voice. "Mr. Barnes, are you trying to tell me that I'm penniless? That I have no home nor any source of income?"

Lawyer Barnes' mouth sagged. "Mercy, I'm sorry. But Flora isn't heartless." He tried to sound optimistic. "I'm sure she'll allow you to remain in your home."

I wondered aloud, still incredulous, "Why did you wait until now to tell me of my position? Joe died last December."

Mr. Barnes dug out a dingy handkerchief and wiped his brow. "I just figured it would be more advantageous for all concerned if neither you nor Flora knew the contents of that blasted will. Shelby and I decided, for the time being, to just let you draw on the family account at the bank. I should have put more pressure on Joe. He never was one to think for himself. And he was only twenty-five, . . . " he finished, as though that explained everything.

I shuddered. "And now Elmer Swindley is courting Flora. And oh, Mr. Barnes, she's swallowing it hook, line and sinker!"

Mr. Barnes leaned over the clutter on his desk and flipped his handkerchief at me. "I know, Mercy. How he found out that Flora is sole heir to the Bishop estate is beyond me. But lawyers have access to things like that. I'm afraid that scoundrel is finally showing his true colors. He'll not rest until he has all your father's assets in his name."

Dazed, I departed from that oven-like room and perspiring old man. For the first time in twenty-three years I limped up the slight incline to Bishop Lane without appreciating the broad tree-lined street with its neatly clipped lawns and rainbow-hued flower beds. And for the first time I stepped between the urn-topped gateposts that allowed entry to the hedged lawns of the Bishop house without feeling enveloped by a sense of privacy.

Inside the front door, I lost any hope of regaining a feeling of refuge in my home. Elmer Swindley was there. As I removed my hat and gloves, a damp hand fell on the nape of my neck and startled a squeal from me. The body attached to the hand slithered around in front of me. Elmer Swindley's bug eyes and twitching lips were inches from my face.

Instinctively I stepped back.

"My dear, aren't you going to congratulate me?" he asked in an oily voice.

I shoved his hand from my shoulder and glared. "I'll thank you to keep your hands to yourself!"

Elmer smirked. "Did anyone ever tell you that those big green eyes shoot sparks? Now, we must be friends. After all, we'll soon be sharing the same roof, my dear. Flora has accepted my proposal of marriage. We've agreed that the engagement period should be brief."

In spite of Lawyer Barnes' disclosure, hearing the words from my enemy's lips left me feeling as unsettled as if he'd yanked the oriental rug from beneath my feet.

I turned and fled up the stairs. Behind the closed

door of my room, I flung myself across my bed and gave way to despair. How could God allow this to happen? First, He'd taken away my protectors, Father and Joe. And now—now my very home was being snatched from me! Even if Flora *would* let me stay, I'd rather live in a cage of snakes than with Elmer Swindley! No doubt the snakes would be safer, too.

But where could I live? Aunt Dolly's good, plain face popped into my mind. No! I couldn't do that to her. She'd given the best years of her life raising Joe and me after Mama's death. And now that she finally had her own little home with Uncle Charlie, she didn't need a maiden niece on her hands.

But I would have to leave quickly. Perhaps I could rent a room and support myself by acquiring more piano students. With this thought, I crawled from the bed and limped to my oak dresser. Lifting the lid of the padded music box, I counted my hoard of silver. The money gave out long before the tune, "Twinkle, Twinkle, Little Star." And this repre- sented six years' savings from piano teaching.

I dropped the coins back into the box and tried to think of another possibility. To whom could I turn? The word, *turn*, pricked my mind. Pastor Wainwright had preached a rousing sermon on turning to God the previous Sunday. With that fine advice ringing in my ears, I picked up my Bible from the bedside table and, in so doing, dislodged a scrap of paper. As I caught it in midair, I recognized it as the letter from Flora's magazine. *A Christian gentleman desires to share his home with a God-fearing wife.* I clutched at the idea like a drowning man to a life preserver. I began composing the letter on the way to my desk.

Somehow the uneasy days had crawled by and once again I was tucked away in my bedroom. This time, praise God, with a letter that solved all my problems. And not a minute too soon! Ignoring the customary mourning period, Elmer and Flora had announced September 16th as their wedding date.

I twirled around on my good leg until two hairpins slipped from my heavy brown bun. With this letter, the axe that hung over my neck no longer threatened. A wonderful man who would care for me all of my life had unwittingly wrenched it from Elmer's hands.

Stashing the letter and clipping in my handbag, I gave my bun a poke and a punch, and fairly flew out of the house and through the streets to Aunt Dolly's house across the tracks. I arrived breathless. Aunt Dolly swept open the screen door before I could collect myself.

"Mercy, child, whatever ails you! Running in this heat. Come in out of the sun," she ordered as she steered me toward a wooden rocker in her tiny doily-festooned sitting room. "Let me get you a drink of water."

I collapsed into the chair, while darting pains stabbed in my crippled hip and leg.

Aunt Dolly returned with the water, her forehead creased with worry lines. I briefly explained the reason for my visit, and Aunt Dolly's thoughts spilled out immediately.

"I blame myself. I knowed things weren't goin' good for you. I'd talked to Lawyer Barnes and of course I'd seen which way the wind blew with that silly Flora."

Sipping on the cool drink, I nearly choked in my

haste to reassure Aunt Dolly. "Oh, Aunt Dolly, don't worry. My problems are all solved. I've found a Christian man to take care of me."

Speechless, Aunt Dolly flopped into another rocker.

Finally she said, "A man, glory be! I shoulda listened to Charlie. Charlie says, 'Let's invite Mercy to live with us. I'll finish off that attic room.' But no, dunce that I be, I says, 'Charlie, Mercy's twenty-three years old and it's high time she stood on her own two feet. Let's just set back and see what direction God points her.' But a man...."

For the first time in weeks I laughed. Aunt Dolly made the most amusing picture—a plump, middle-aged woman with her mouth hanging open and her arms sagging limply over the chair arms.

"What's the matter, Aunt Dolly? Don't you believe a man would want me?" I teased.

Aunt Dolly sprang to life. "Mercy, don't you think that! Glory be, you coulda had a man years ago with your smart looks—great big green eyes and that pile of hair. No, the trouble was your pa, God rest his soul, and he bein' my own brother. But that man always had to be the one, yes, the *one*."

"Aunt Dolly, how can you say that?" I protested. "Father spent his life caring for me and the rest of the family. I think he suffered all his days, blaming himself for not catching me before I crawled into the stall with that temperamental horse that kicked me and ruined my hip when I was just two. He'd have kept on taking care of you, too, if you hadn't married Charlie after his mother died."

Aunt Dolly chewed her lip. "Maybe I shouldn't tell you this, but you're grown now so I will," she decided. "Your pa raised the roof when I told him about marryin' Charlie and movin' across the tracks to his house. He never could see anybody wanting a life of their own. With Joe marrying Flora and you grown, you didn't need me in that shrine your pa built. I loved Charlie and no kitchen is big enough for two women, not even your father's kitchen."

I didn't feel up to arguing with Aunt Dolly about my father so I fell on her last words. "Which is why I knew I couldn't move in with you."

I pulled the clipping and letter from my handbag and handed them to Aunt Dolly. "After you read the clipping and letter, you'll see how God has rescued me."

Aunt Dolly held the articles at arm's length so her farsighted eyes could make out the fine print. Silently she returned the two pieces of paper. Then she leaned back and studied me until I squirmed and searched for something to say.

Finally Aunt Dolly spoke. "Specks I'm plumb crazy to say this but, Mercy, I say you should go. Now mind," she bent over and shook her finger for emphasis, "I'm not saying that you should marry that Levi Miller even if he does claim to be a Christian. Some folks claim to be Christians but ain't never trusted in Christ's shed blood, and some have but don't act like it at all. That man seems to toot his own horn too much for my liking. But Mercy, you gotta grow up, stop leanin' on mortals and take to trustin' God more. Your pa treated you like an empty-headed doll, but you got brains. Use 'em. And if this Levi Miller ain't a man you can love and cherish, look around. By the by, can you put your hands on some money?"

By the time Aunt Dolly had finished her lecture, I

could barely contain myself. "Oh yes, Aunt Dolly! I've been wanting to tell you all the plans I've made ever since I wrote the letter, but something held me back. What if he hadn't picked me? I hope he's not disappointed. I was less than honest, I'm afraid. I told him about knowing the Lord and teaching the Infants' Class at church but I couldn't bring myself to tell him about my weak leg and my foolish fear of horses. Do you think he'll be sorry he chose me?"

"Now, I doubt that, Mercy. But you've got to be able to take care of yourself if this crazy scheme don't work out."

"Well, you can rest assured I'll have enough to get me there and carry me through for a short time. I went over everything with Mr. Barnes after I sent my letter off. I'm selling my bedroom set and most of Mama's jewelry. Mr. Barnes says Flora hasn't any claim on those. I'm keeping the gold locket with Mama's and Father's pictures in it and you will have the pearls."

Aunt Dolly raised her hand. "Now, Mercy, don't you be giving me your mama's pearls."

"Yes, I will," I insisted. "They'll look nice on your Sunday dresses. And the grand piano Father bought me goes to Sarah James. She's my most faithful student and the Jameses will never be able to afford one."

Aunt Dolly chuckled. "Good for you, girl. Elmer'll no doubt have conniptions about losing a valuable piano, but serves 'im right. Appears you'll have enough to get you settled."

"Oh, Aunt Dolly," I said jubilantly "It's so much fun telling you everything! Don't you think Mr. Miller sounds strong and capable?"

Aunt Dolly sighed. "Mercy, you make sure that man is godly first. Now Uncle Charlie ain't a man to make a woman's heart do flip-flops, but he's kind, big-hearted, don't never tell a lie nor go flyin' off the handle. And you can trust him with all your heart. You get a man like that."

I kept my opinion of Uncle Charlie to myself. Aunt Dolly spoke the truth as far as it went, but her love blinded her to his pig-in-the-parlor manners. Thank goodness Levi Miller's refined ways just oozed from his letter.

Aunt Dolly cut into my thoughts with, "Speakin' of Charlie, that man will be a-coming through the door any minute wanting supper and here I ain't got it underway."

She heaved herself up out of her chair. "By the by, you get your train ticket first thing. Count on me to help you pack your trunks. I'll rest easier once you're outa that house. Elmer can't be trusted no more than a skunk in a hen house."

I jumped up and buried my nose in her apron top. It smelled like freshly baked bread. "Oh, I do hope I'm doing the right thing."

"Glory be!" Aunt Dolly patted my back. "Every woman needs a little nest of her own. You just let God do the pointing. Montana's a far piece, but not so far God ain't there. No way I'd rest easy if I weren't sure you should go."

Nothing in my previous life as the daughter of one of Oak Grove's leading citizens had prepared me for the days just prior to my departure. Each person reacted differently to the astonishing news that the retiring Miss Mercy Bishop planned marriage to a man in remote Montana.

While Flora couldn't quite cover her relief, Elmer

expressed unctuous regret, "Mercy, you aren't serious! Flora and I had looked forward to you making your home with us."

"We must give a tea in your honor," a mother of one of the children in my Infants' Class planned. "How we'll replace you, I can't imagine."

A former classmate was more candid than most. "Mercy, is it true you're leaving your great big, fancy home and moving to Montana? But like I told my Mister, you tell me who'd live under the same roof with that Elmer Swindley. And to think, I envied you when we were in school."

Except for Aunt Dolly, parting with the James' children was the most difficult.

"Mercy, I'll simply wither and die without you next door. But I love my piano. Thank you, thank you!" Sarah gushed.

"Here's a real sharp Bowie knife. I hear the Indians are mighty thick in Montana. Soon as I grow up, I'm a-comin' out. I'll look you up," Buster exclaimed protectively.

Quicker than I could scream, "No! I've changed my mind," the date on the ticket corresponded with the date on the calendar.

Aunt Dolly fussed about the early departure time. "Can't see why you need to leave in the middle of the night. And glory be, Mercy, you keep that money belt next to your skin. You ain't got any too much to spare."

I knew Aunt Dolly found my leaving a bitter pill to swallow, but privately I thanked the Lord I'd had enough sense to schedule my leavetaking in the pre-dawn darkness when the depot was empty.

This way no one but Uncle Charlie and Aunt Dolly were present to witness the shambles I made of my farewells. First, Uncle Charlie stepped forward and snapped his suspenders. "Mercy, we got all your trunks ticketed through to Prospect. Now you give your Uncle Charlie a hug and we'll come see you when we strike it rich. Hee, Hee."

Then I barely had time to throw my arms around Aunt Dolly. Wrenching myself from her tight embrace, I stumbled up the train steps with tears clouding my vision. It wasn't until I'd plopped into an empty seat that I found my handkerchief and dabbed at my eyes. But the fountain wouldn't dry up and soon Uncle Charlie and Aunt Dolly were fuzzy blobs standing beneath the feeble kerosene light standards of Oak Grove's depot.

As the train lurched to a start, I whispered into the darkness of the coach, "I'm all alone now, Lord. I've no one but you."

With that prayer barely off my lips, I pummeled my pillow into a satisfactory shape, dropped my weary head into its downy depths and drifted into blessed oblivion.

Chapter 2

Still deep in sleep, I attempted to shrug off the slight tap on my shoulder, but a soft, slurring voice refused to allow me to nestle further into my pillow. "Ticket please, Ma'am."

Lifting heavy lids, my eyes focused on two rows of silver buttons marching up a black coat. I followed the buttons upward to a velvety black face split in half by a white grin.

"Why, hello," I said drowsily.

"Ma'am, I sure do hates to wake you. I left you to the last but I needs to punch your ticket before the end of the line in St. Paul."

"Oh, my gracious, I've been asleep for hours then," I said in surprise, plunging into my handbag for my ticket.

The conductor had just turned his broad back when a scrap of a child popped around the edge of my seat. Her thick black hair was cut bluntly over her eyes and just under her ears. Large blue eyes seemed to barely leave room on her face for a snub nose and an impish mouth.

"Howdy-do," the small figure in a smudged blue dress said while she edged into the seat beside me. "I didn't like sitting with that old man. So I'll just sit here."

"Oh," I responded, wiping the sleep from my eyes.

Blue eyes studied me. "Why don't you push your hat off your face?"

I touched my hat brim. "Oh dear, I'm afraid I forgot to remove it before I fell asleep. I must look a fright."

The little girl watched intently while I pushed stray hairs into the heavy bun on my neck and twisted the gray skirt of my traveling suit into line. Aunt Dolly had persuaded me to discard traditional mourning clothes in favor of something more practical for my trip. "Black shows every speck," she'd reasoned.

"You look like a real lady," my small companion observed. "I'm going to St. Paul to live with my Aunt Bess. Where are you going?"

For one awful moment I couldn't recall my destination. Then the impact of what I was doing rocked me fully awake. With every click of the rails this great iron monster bore me further from home. A quick glance at the landscape flashing past my window produced the same 'gone' feeling I'd had when Aunt Dolly left me, a tiny six-year-old, at the school door on opening day. I felt just as adrift today as I had that day. Was leaving my home really my only choice? A brief stab of homesickness attacked before I could square my shoulders against a further onslaught. Leaving the past behind, I answered the child's question.

"I'm on my way to Prospect, Montana."

"Where's that?" the questionbox asked.

Instead of answering, I thumbed through the contents of my handbag until I located my new and up-to-date Rand McNally Map of the United States. I'd pored over the route to Prospect so many times in the past week that smoothing out the tricky creases was like child's play. Without hesitation I pointed to the speck that indicated Prospect, located in the County of Missoula on the western border of the vast state of Montana.

Gazing at those eight letters on the map brought my future out of the clouds and back to reality. On that exact spot of the world a man awaited my arrival. Was he anxious, as he had said in his letter? Would he be happy with his choice? Would he be handsome and well-groomed like the men in my life had always been? I didn't think I could tolerate a smelly man.

A kick on the ankle, delivered by my neighbor's scruffy toe, ended my daydreaming. "Don't you smell fried chicken? I do, and I think it's coming from that basket on the floor."

I inhaled. "Now that you mention it, I smell a number of odors, but not all are from my lunch basket. Someone in this car is smoking a cigar, I'm sure, and somebody has fish in their lunch. And boiled eggs. I'm sure I detect the aroma of a boiled egg."

Tired of being put off, the little girl insisted, "But I'm hungry and I smell chicken in *your* basket."

Silently wishing Aunt Bess success in teaching the youngster manners, I answered, "Before we eat together I think we should be properly introduced.

I'm Miss Mercy Bishop and what might your name be?"

With her eyes fixed on the seat back in front of us she said, "When my granny put me on the train she told me not to tell strangers my name."

"I beg your pardon. I'm sure your granny wouldn't want you to accept food from a stranger then, either," I said with a grin.

She slumped into her seat and studied her nail-bitten fingers. Then she lifted her head and looked directly into my eyes. "Guess we won't be strangers if you know my name and I know yours. I'm Miss Harriet Bothwell."

"Pleased to meet you, Miss Harriet. Now, let's see what my Aunt Dolly packed in this lunch hamper. I'm hungry enough to eat a horse, but I'm sure you're right and it's chicken we smell."

During the next moments I had reason to question the wisdom of carrying chicken on train journeys. Harriet attacked the crispy chicken like a starved dog, flinging grease everywhere. After the chicken had been reduced to a pile of bones, I mopped at the spots on Harriet's face and hands. I ignored the dingy dress. By the time we reached St. Paul, no one would be able to discern the former stains from the latter, I reasoned.

Next we shared bread and butter, finishing our meal with cookies and apples. Then, pleasantly stuffed, we made our way to the washroom.

Harriet skipped along between the seats, but always conscious of my poor balance, I carefully placed one foot in front of the other while clutching the seat backs with stiff fingers. Several passengers turned as I inched forward. Giving them a weak smile, I wished fervently that they wouldn't stare.

By the time I eased into my seat again, I felt as though I'd made a trip to an alien country instead of the back of the car. I blessed Mr. Pullman or whoever was responsible for the privacy offered by the tall seat backs.

Harriet's return journey included so many detours that I'd filled the message side of two postal cards, one to Aunt Dolly and one to the James children, before she returned. The train abounded with hawkers and I'd purchased the scenic cards from a passing newsboy for a penny.

Somewhere along the line Harriet had collected a chocolate smear on the cheek I'd recently scrubbed in the washroom.

"I like riding the train. Do you think Aunt Bess will send me back to Granny?"

"I should hope you'd be such a good child that your Aunt Bess wouldn't want to part from you," I said piously.

Being good reminded me of the Bible cards stashed away in my wicker bag. I'd found the pictures of Bible scenes most effective in my Infants' Class. Fishing them out, I propped them on the arm rest and proceeded to describe the illustrated events to Harriet. To my dismay, she asked the most outlandish questions, then yawned broadly, saying, "I'm like my Granny. Religion don't stick with us."

I repacked the cards with less than a charitable attitude. So much for missionary endeavors. Twisting toward the window, I counted telegraph poles in the gathering dusk until I could again turn to Harriet in kindness.

By then she had rolled into a little ball and was fast asleep. While tucking her hem around her exposed knees, I became aware of an air of activity pervading the car. Fellow passengers were dragging luggage off the overhead racks and rescuing belongings from underfoot. Just as I pulled myself to my feet for a better view, the conductor with the shiny buttons reappeared. "St. Paul, next stop."

I gasped. This meant I must somehow transfer myself and all my trappings from this train to the one heading west to Fargo, North Dakota. I'd trust the railway to see to my ticketed trunks.

Afterward, the St. Paul depot, which was so big Oak Grove's could have hidden in its ticket office, was only a hectic blur in my memory. It was a sea of humanity, all set on different courses, wasting no time in scurrying to reach their destinations.

I'd propelled Harriet into motion before setting forth on my own course. My last glimpse of that determined little girl was of her darned black stockings as she dove into the aisle to retrieve her belongings from the first seat she'd occupied.

I didn't give her another thought until I'd deposited myself and assorted bags on the "points west" train. After congratulating myself on successfully navigating the strange depot, my conscience gave me a little nudge. But nothing short of a knife in my back would have induced me to expose my shaky hip to the hazards of that crowded station again. I satisfied myself with the thought that anyone as aggressive as Harriet could undoubtedly locate her Aunt Bess without my help.

A large woman in a deep plum coat brought me out of my reverie. "Young lady, would you remove your things so I can sit down." It was a demand rather than a question.

"Sorry," I mumbled as I stashed my basket and bags under my feet.

Lowering herself into the seat, she informed me, "You could stick them on the rack over your head."

"No, thank you."

"Well, suit yourself. I'm Mrs. Bertram on my way to Fargo. My daughter broke her leg and I'm going out to see her family. She's got a husband that don't know his right hand from his left and three children that take after his side of the family."

"Oh."

Mrs. Bertram settled into her seat like one of Aunt Dolly's broody hens. "Where're you headed?" she asked.

Before I could frame an answer, the train shuddered into motion and the conductor, looking like a twin to the one on the train from Iowa, made his way down the aisle, snapping his ticket punch and lighting the lamps.

Mrs. Bertram soon lost interest in someone as trifling as I and struck up a conversation across the aisle. I found myself nodding off.

Throughout the night the measured clicking of the rails lulled me into dreamland. But repeatedly a number of things snatched me back to the reality of my surroundings. No matter which way I shifted on the hard, scratchy seat, some part of my anatomy protested after an hour or so. Either my hip or arm or maybe just a toe became prickly numb and goaded me into rearranging my body.

Also, never before had I shared my bedroom. Now at least two dozen bodies were within spitting distance (to quote Uncle Charlie) in my traveling boudoir. And no one slept quietly. If it wasn't a baby fussing, somebody hacked, whispered, muttered or snored.

The further the night advanced, the more

33

frequently my nose aroused me. The aroma of perspiring bodies, dirty diapers, stale food and other questionable odors could first be described as heady, then pungent and finally suffocating. Stuffing my lavendar-scented handkerchief beneath my nose proved effective until I relaxed and it fell to my lap.

Earlier, a heated discussion had transpired between the occupants of the seat in front of me, a husband and wife I gathered, concerning the pros and cons of opening the window. The pros won until a chilly blast whipped in a liberal coating of coal dust from the smokestack.

In one of my wakeful moments, I wished myself back into my soft, broad bed between sheets smelling of fresh air, with a perfume-laden breeze fingering the lace curtains.

I hesitated to even admit it to myself but I was homesick again. I alternated between anticipation of my new life and despair that everything familiar to me was irretrievable. However, I pulled this longing up short by forcing my mind to picture Elmer Swindley enthroned in the master suite while I cowered in my room with a deadbolt lock securing the door.

With the coming of the new day, I lost my seatmate. Her deep plum figure faded into the dim light of dawn as the train shuddered to a stop. According to the conductor, we were in Fargo, North Dakota and were advised to take advantage of the railroad dining room.

Because I avoided crowds whenever I possibly could, I retrieved my lunch basket and made my breakfast out of stale leftovers. I washed them down with lukewarm coffee purchased from a passing vendor. It cost a small fortune and was bitter to boot, but better a complaining stomach than risk losing my balance far from the safety of my seat.

After the aisles had cleared, I made the most of the stopover and used the washroom. The girl that peeked back from the mottled mirror with anxious green eyes was covered with a fine layer of dust. I repressed my desire to scrub furiously, don a fresh set of clothes, and draw a brush through my hair. I did what I could with the scanty water supply and promised myself I'd repair the damage before meeting Mr. Miller in Prospect. Even after that discouraging assessment, I scuttled back to my seat greatly refreshed.

After we pulled out of Fargo, I gave my attention to studying the landscape flashing past my window. It did nothing to reassure me. In my opinion, North Dakota had too much of nothing. I preferred the friendly groves of trees, streams, and fence lines of Iowa. Here the uneven plains covered with tall, restless grass went on forever, only rarely relieved by some underdeveloped-looking trees or a house dwarfed by its surroundings. Every hour or so one might catch sight of grazing cattle or a band of sheep presided over by a herder atop a horse.

If the flag was out along the tracks or a passenger wanted off, our train whistled sharply, pitched, jerked and ground to another stop. The further west we advanced, the larger the numbers identifying railroad sidings became and the smaller the clusters of buildings. Sometimes a siding consisted only of a lone water tower.

As the day wore on, the seat next to me remained vacant. With the quiet a welcome relief, I spent the time reading the Psalms. Psalm 121, where David shared his thoughts concerning mountains, especially appealed to me since I eagerly awaited my first glimpse of the western mountains. I prayed they'd be more appealing than this area labeled on my map as the "great plains."

The words, "But my help cometh from the Lord who made heaven and earth" jumped out at me. Perhaps I needed to be reminded where to look for help. Not from mountains, nor people, nor any created thing, but from God, I mused, as the train lurched to a stop.

It was the tenth siding and one woman boarded. She came into view over the seat back of the row in front of me. Two large purple roses drooping over the brim of a tattered straw hat first caught my eye. They looked right at home on a stack of hair resembling an abandoned bird's nest. Then my eyes met hers. They were a warm, friendly brown.

She stopped. "You're the first alone woman I've seen on this here train, so I'll just set myself down."

She flopped into the seat and maneuvered a large, twine-wrapped cardboard carton onto her lap. Soon she twisted around to face me and said, "I could tell right off that me and you'd like each other. I'm Emmylou Brown." She shoved a work-roughened hand in my face.

I hesitated. Ladies didn't normally shake hands, but from our brief acquaintance I'd already concluded that my new seatmate wasn't a lady. I gave her the tip of my gloved fingers and politely murmured, "I'm pleased to meet you. I'm Miss Mercy Bishop."

She threw her head back and roared, revealing several gaps in her teeth. "Honey, ya don't need to call yourself Miss to me. It sticks out all over ya that ya ain't had no truck with men. It's jest as plain as can be that you've been tucked up in cotton wool ever since ya first opened them big green eyes of yours."

At this outburst, I tried to shrink into the crack between the seat and the outside wall. Boldly she leaned over her box until the brim of her hat brushed my forehead. A waft of foul air accompanied this movement. She patted my arm and assured me, "Don't let that faze ya none. Ya ain't to blame fer bein' mollycoddled no more'n I am fer all but gettin' tossed out with the birthin' water."

I was so relieved when she settled back into her seat that I turned a deaf ear to her words. Only good manners kept me from fanning the air. Silently, I looked down my freckled nose at the gap in her shirtwaist. Surely she could have managed a button! Unless, heaven forbid, she wanted strangers peering at her grimy corset.

Oblivious to my disapproving scrutiny, Emmylou slapped the top of the box in her lap and said, "Men! Cain't git along with 'em nor without 'em. The last one of mine were so dirty-dog mean, I'd be six foot under this here minute if'n I hadn't a-got to the gun first."

"M-m-murder?" I stammered.

"Yup, but the jury seen it my way. That lawyer feller told me they'd always side with a purty face," she said as she cocked her head to one side and seemed to reflect on what I assumed must be a wicked and violent past. I turned away, not wanting any part of a murderess.

She yanked herself back to the present, though, and jabbed me with her elbow. "I'm a-startin' all over agin out in Montana. Where ya headed?"

I paused, torn between pity for a woman forced to murder her husband and an urge to crawl into my shell. But I couldn't be rude, so I answered without quite looking into her eyes.

"I'm going to Montana also." Then, because that seemed a bit short, I added, "I'm going to be married to a rancher there."

She bounced around in excitement. "Well, I'll be blamed! So am I. I been hitched up three times. Two times to bums and once to a feller that up and died—too good for this world. I'm a-marryin' a Christian this time. The sheriff's wife, who ar an angel if I ever saw one, put me on to this feller. Ya see, I had to stay with her after they arrested me since the jailhouse had a man in it. Anyhow, Mrs. Cameron—that being her name—read about this feller in one of her papers. She was a great one fer reading."

While Mrs. Brown babbled on, I felt a faint stirring in the back of my mind. There was something altogether too familiar about her story. The stirring agitated into a whirlwind as she continued.

"So's Mrs. Cameron helped me to write to this gent and I'll be blamed if he didn't write back and want me to come out and marry him. Someways Mrs. Cameron layed her hands on enough money to get me to Prospect."

The whirlwind threatened to remove the top of my head. I placed a trembling hand on Mrs. Brown's arm. She stopped her monologue and looked at me sheepishly. "I'm a-workin' my jaw too much. Happens every blamed time I get within shoutin' distance of a lady, but . . . . "

"Please," I asked, praying my suspicions were wrong. "What's the man's name?"

Mrs. Brown's eyebrows lifted in surprise. "First off was Zeb Freeman. No better'n a skunk. He vamoosed while I was with childbed fever. After that I hitched up with Hank Duffy and he died on me—too good for this world. After ..."

Resisting the urge to scream, I begged, "No, no. Please tell me the name of the man who wrote for you to come to Prospect and marry him."

"Oh, him. Hold your taters," she said agreeably while she poked around in the pocket of her threadbare jacket. She fished out a folded paper. While she flipped it open and spread it out, I held my breath. "I can't make out readin' much, but his name is Miller."

With that devastating piece of news, she handed me a letter that matched the one resting in my handbag—word for word.

Chapter 3

Swimming up from what seemed like a thick fog, I wondered who'd opened the train window. Rapidly moving air lifted the collar of my shirtwaist and stirred the lapels of my jacket. As my eyes began to focus, something clipped the end of my nose.

"I'll be blamed," Mrs. Brown was muttering while vigorously fanning my face with the letter.

"If ya didn't scare the socks off me, faintin' away like that! Nothin' to ya but green eyes and a gob of hair. What ya be needin' is a good slug of whiskey. Put some mettle in ya."

I swatted the letter to one side and struggled to get my bearings while Mrs. Brown watched anxiously. "Ya be as white as a dinner plate. I'm a-gonna git ya a drink of water."

Looking back, I'm sure it was the shock that compelled me to unload my burden on an avowed murderess.

Before she had a chance to hand me the water and seat herself again, the words tumbled out. "Mrs. Brown, we're going West to marry the same man."

Her mouth sagged. Two little boys who were chasing each other down the aisle brought her back to life when they bumped into her, spilling the water. Yelling at them, she wiped her wet hand across her skirt and fell down into her seat. Handing me what remained of the water, she demanded, "Now what'd ya say? I'm kinda thick-skulled. Thought ya told me we was both gettin' hitched to that Miller feller."

With trembling lips I sipped the tepid water and avoided looking her way. "And I thought he'd be such a gentleman. Really care for me."

Mrs. Brown grabbed my arm. "Now listen here, Mercy Bishop, ya gotta level with me. I got big shoulders. Are ya a-sayin' that this here Christian gentleman wrote and told ya to come and marry him, too?"

"Mrs. Brown, your letter and mine are the same, word for word," I whispered around the lump in my throat.

Her fingers dug into my arm until I squealed.

"Sorry," she muttered, then she raised her voice and spat out a curse on men everywhere. Crossing her arms, she settled into her seat, and glowered into space.

I couldn't seem to fasten my mind on anything and Mrs. Brown appeared preoccupied, too.

Finally she spoke. "Mercy, get your chin outa your lap and look at me. Me and you got some plannin' to do."

Reluctantly, I looked into her face. This time her

coarseness didn't catch my attention. I saw only the look of concern in her eyes.

"I've been a-cogitatin'," she began. "You'd best skedaddle home. Hop off at the next stop and catch the first train headin' East. I've been a-doin' fer myself ever since I run off at twelve, but I kin tell real plain that the only thing you'd know to do is sit in a parlor and sip tea outa a china cup."

Her assumption irritated me, partly because I was afraid there was more than a little truth to it. "Mrs. Brown!" I couldn't help sounding a bit defensive, even to myself. "I may not have been on my own since I was twelve, but Aunt Dolly trained me in all household tasks, and my father saw that I had a well-rounded education at Miss Prince's Female Academy. I've also given piano lessons for the past six years. But," I finished lamely, "I didn't earn enough to support myself."

Mrs. Brown's lips twitched. "Now don't ya go gettin' on a high horse. I'm not a-tryin' to shove yer face in the mud. I'm just tellin' things as I sees 'em. And stop calling me Mrs. Brown! That were my maiden name. I took it back once I decided to start life again with a clean slate. Thought I'd be Mrs. Miller before long," she added grimly. "Call me Emmylou."

Hearing the disappointment in her voice heightened my own sense of helplessness. "Oh, Emmylou, I can't go home. Elmer Swindley owns it all now."

Naturally Emmylou wanted to know who Elmer Swindley was.

I spent the next half-hour relating the tragic details of my life since Father's death. Emmylou listened intently, interjecting several choice words to express her opinion of Elmer Swindley and men in general. Father and Joe didn't escape her sharp tongue, either.

I ended by saying, "I guess you're right about not trusting entirely in humans. I'm trying to trust God instead, like Aunt Dolly advised me."

Emmylou nearly leapt out of her seat and yelled. "Trust God? Ha! Seems like He musta been sleepin' when ya needed Him."

The man and woman across the aisle looked our way and a pair of bespectacled eyes peeked over the seat in front of us.

I shrank into the corner of my seat and pleaded, "Emmylou, don't raise your voice. A lady never calls attention to herself. And, of course, God wasn't asleep. It's blasphemous to say so. It says in the Psalms that 'He neither slumbers nor sleeps.' "

Not in the least chagrined, Emmylou rapped her calloused knuckles on her knees and announced to anyone who cared to listen, "If He weren't asleep, He musta been lookin' the other way, then."

"Emmylou," I asked, "how could you write Mr. Miller that you were a godly woman?"

Emmylou lowered her voice an octave or so. "Mrs. Cameron writ that letter. I specks she stretched the truth a tad 'cause the only dealings I've had with God is when the preacher said some words over my ma's grave."

"My goodness, no wonder you don't know about God. I've attended church all my life and read my chapter a day since I was eight-years-old. I made a personal commitment to Christ then. Don't worry, Emmylou, I'll teach you," I assured her.

Emmylou's brown eyes twinkled and her mouth broke into a big smile. "Honey, I ain't meanin' to throw cold water on your plans but I'd druther be run over by a train than a lady preacher. What me and you gotta talk over is, do we git off at some likely spot along the way or do we use up our tickets and go through to Prospect like we writ Mr. Miller?"

"I haven't any choice," I decided. "I can't go back and face Elmer Swindley. And Aunt Dolly thinks I need to trust God more and stand on my own two feet. So I won't go back without trying."

"Okay, I'm game fer it, too. It's on to Prospect, then, and let's shake on it," Emmylou suggested.

This time I wrapped all ten of my fingers snugly around the hand she offered me.

After we'd made our decision to continue to Prospect, Emmylou left her seat and seemed to shed her cares like a cloak. Her bedraggled roses bobbed about the railroad car as she scattered goodwill throughout the car.

Taking advantage of her absence, I mumbled some prayers to God, but they seemed to bounce off the baggage rack over my head and drop to the floor. No divine guidance came.

After a time Emmylou paused beside our seat and urged me to socialize with her. Not wanting my physical liability to be public, I motioned for her to sit beside me.

"Emmylou, there are times when I have problems balancing on a steady surface. Walking with the train in motion would undoubtedly throw me on my face. You see, I had an accident when I was two that left me with a damaged hip."

Emmylou insisted on knowing all the details of my accident with the horse. After reciting them to her, she laid her hand on my arm and said, "Now Mercy, don't ya fret none. Course ya wouldn't be knowing, but I be a doctor."

My astonishment must have shown for she continued, "Yup, I lived within a stone's throw of an old Indian squaw that were a doctor to her people and she larned me all she knowed. Stowed away in that box of mine be just the cure fer achin' hips. I'll take care of it once we land in Prospect."

I looked at her dirt-encrusted fingernails resting on the white ruffle of my sleeve and shuddered. Suddenly she pointed out the window and squealed, "Lookee thar, Mercy. Did ya ever lay eyes on so many antelope?"

Hundreds of tawny animals, looking no bigger than rabbits from this distance, skimmed across the broken prairie. I marvelled at their effortless speed.

"They go mighty good in a stew pot, too," Emmylou informed me.

I wrinkled my nose, then changed the subject. "Emmylou, I've always thought red checkered curtains and a matching tablecloth looked homey in a kitchen. I must confess I'd dreamed about furnishing my ranch kitchen with them. I even packed them in one of my trunks."

Emmylou chuckled. "Mercy, me and you's about as mismatched as a mule and a thoroughbred. Me, I'd jest thank my lucky stars to cook under a roof that don't leak. Every blamed shack I ever lived in had a leaky roof."

"I can't imagine where we'll live when we get to Prospect," I worried. "I haven't enough money to stay in a hotel for long."

"I promise ya one thing, Mercy. If I ever get my hands on that low-down, double-crossing Levi Miller, I'll wring his neck."

46

Her promise did little to ease my anxious thoughts.

It would take two more days for our train to wind around and over the uneven terrain and chug into Missoula, the change point. But my new circumstances wrung much of the joy out of my first sight of the Montana mountains. Not even the green tree-covered slopes plunging down to sparkling streams lifted my spirits.

And instead of Emmylou's cheerful attitude encouraging me, I found it annoying. I longed for solitude, a chance to stroll on solid ground, fresh air to fill my lungs, a long soak in a hot bath, and something in my stomach besides the heavy, greasy food available at the railway dinner stops. I'm ashamed to admit it, but instead of meditating on Scripture I gazed gloomily out the window and examined my miseries from every angle. It's certain that Emmylou didn't see the Biblical commands, "Rejoice in the Lord always" or "In everything give thanks," in my deportment.

Finally, on a lovely September evening our train shuddered to a standstill in Missoula, Montana.

We'd spend the night in this little town laid out along a river, the same river that The Local followed. The Local was the train that made a trip every other day through the mountain country northwest to Wallace, Idaho. Somewhere between here and there, if what the gossip Emmylou had gleaned could be trusted, was Prospect.

Two things about our overnight stay in Missoula stand out in my memory.

The first is the restorative power of 25¢ worth of steamy, delightful water cascading over my travel-worn body. That and a full bar of castile soap made a new woman of me. The young lady that waltzed out of Mrs. Tucker's Modern Bath House looked like the "after" of a vitamin advertisement, as surely as the woman who'd staggered in resembled the "before."

My second memorable event was most unsettling. When I returned to the hotel room we'd rented for the night, I discovered Emmylou flopped across the bed, spread-eagled. Little snorting noises escaped through her lips as she slept. By all appearances, she hadn't even concerned herself with so much as a sponge bath, and she still wore the same dingy skirt and waist, minus one button. The scuffed toes of her shoes pointed toward the ceiling.

I forcibly halted the uncharitable thoughts which were marching through my mind. After all, whose muscled arm had guided me off the train? Whose friendly smile had secured the information as to the best hotel while I sagged alongside like a hundred-year-old grandma?

I pulled a fresh nighty over my damp, squeaky-clean hair. As I shoved Emmylou to one side, I brushed all thoughts of her grooming habits from my mind. Exhaustion claimed me. I slipped between the sheets and joined her in dreamland before any foul smells wafted across the bedcovers to tickle my nose.

Emmylou's rummaging in her box awoke me the next morning. I peeked over the end of the bed, curious as to what her one piece of baggage held.

The creaking of the bedsprings caused her to look up. "Morning, Mercy, this here's our big day."

"Emmylou, what do all those little cloth bags hold? They smell like the apothecary section of a drugstore," I said as I watched her dig through a large pile of plump fabric bags.

"Why, honey," she exclaimed, "this here's my herbs. I told ya I be a doctor. I was a-lookin' them over to make sure they ain't spoiled or nothin'. There may not be a doctor in Prospect."

Her mention of Prospect whirled me into action. I jumped from bed, sponged off my traveling suit and extracted a crisp, white, ruffled shirtwaist from the one trunk I'd had delivered to my room. I laid out fresh undergarments and hummed while I buffed the long narrow toes of my shoes to a mirror finish. Using the mirror over the bureau, I completed my toilet by adjusting my hat at a jaunty tilt, just as Emmylou slapped the cover on her box.

Our eyes met in the mirror. "I'll be blamed, Mercy, ya take more bother gettin' gussied up than if ya was going to meet the President."

A silent moment passed while I studied her in the mirror. Her merry brown eyes and dimpled cheeks convinced me that her remark wasn't meant to be unkind.

She can poke fun of me if she likes, I thought, but I failed to see any humor in her sloppy habits. How an adult could be so unaware of her appearance was past my understanding. I searched for words of admonition but before I could string together any that wouldn't sound offensive she had grabbed the twine to tie her box and planned aloud.

"We'd best git our trappin's together and grab a bite. Train leaves at nine sharp."

As our engine, with its two passenger cars trailing behind, puffed out of Missoula and into the majestic scenery, I retreated behind the covers of my Bible.

A reference about mountains had been plaguing me. I searched through the black book until I located the passage in Matthew. "If ye have faith as a grain of mustard seed, ye shall say unto the mountain, remove hence to yonder place, and it shall remove; and nothing shall be impossible unto ye."

From some unremembered past, I had penned a reference beside the verse. Flipping to Hebrews 11:1, I read, "Now faith is the substance of things hoped for, the evidence of things not seen."

I looked away from my Bible to the mountains just beyond the train window. Certainly these weren't the mountains I hoped to see removed. Their magnificence drew me out of myself. But fear loomed in front of me like an insurmountable mountain. Fear of the unknown, of how I'd care for myself, of strangers ... and, oddly enough, fear of Levi Miller whose protective cloak had been yanked from me. Whatever did a lady say to a man who had deceived her?

Glancing at the Hebrews verse, I could say I *hoped* with God's help to overcome my mountain-high fears.

I emerged from my spiritual ramblings to hear a loud, raspy voice say, "The railroad opened up this here part of the country. Before that, there was nothing but trails the gold miners and Mr. Mullan put through."

Across the aisle, a man whose stiff gray whiskers reminded me of an elderly porcupine had captured Emmylou's attention. Evidently age had impaired his sense of hearing for he had one volume—loud.

"Yes sir, miss," he roared, "With this railroad and

50

the tracks being laid fer another one, towns are being built all through these here mountains. I foresee every mother's son pushin' in. There's silver, lead and zinc up to Iron Mountain. If ya ain't of the persuasion to mine gold or ore, the railroad's paying good for ties and the Cyr brothers opened up a sawmill on Cedar Creek. Why, when I were a pup, only way into this country were on horse and . . . . "

Closing my ears to Mr. Whisker's oration, I let myself be immersed in the picture outside my window. Our little train followed its tracks through a small valley town. Then it hugged a mountain of pines and towering peaks while crossing a river innumerable times. The river snaked along the bottom of a gorge many feet below the train trestle. Although the train fearlessly chugged across these trestles made of a network of poles, my heart skipped a beat or two every time.

In early afternoon, our engine steamed around a bend to a small mountain meadow. The flat land melted into the inevitable mountains on three sides, with the railroad and river on the fourth.

Stretched out along the tracks were a handful of rough buildings. The train whistle announced our arrival, as the even beat of our wheels slowed their tempo, then squealed to a stop alongside a building resembling an unpainted chicken coop.

The bold white letters on its side read, PROSPECT.

Chapter 4

No impatient bridegroom hurried forward as we stepped from the train. As a matter of fact, *no one* met the train. Inwardly, I gave thanks. This would give me time to adjust to my surroundings.

Before returning to the train, the conductor unlocked the door to the ticket office and tossed the mail bag inside. He told us the ticket agent would arrive in due time, and reboarded the train. The brakes were released and the train rumbled into motion, leaving us amidst my three large trunks. After the train disappeared around a curve, we could have been alone in a painted landscape, the stillness was so complete.

Emmylou settled on a trunk top while I surveyed our surroundings. When God had created this nook of the world He'd done things in a big way, I thought. Vivid greens, sharp angles and a broad river beneath an azure sky revealed the string of motley buildings for what they were, trifling.

"For what is man that thou art mindful of him," I quoted softly.

"I'll be blamed, Mercy, if this here mountain air ain't turning your brains. Mumbling to yourself," Emmylou said, as she waved her hand in front of my eyes. "I were just a-thinkin'. Fer sounding so desperate, that two-timing gent don't seem in much of a rush to meet his bride."

Leave it to Emmylou to bring a person back to earth, I thought resentfully. "Emmylou, I do hope you won't tell everyone in this little town why we've come—will you?"

"Ya bet your boots we'll keep our traps shut." Emmylou retorted vigorously. "The best way to nab an enemy is sneak up on him. Far as the locals are concerned, we's just a traipsin' around the country."

Without warning, a youthful voice sang out from the other side of the ticket office. "Howdy do."

A stocky twelve- or thirteen-year-old, with a snub nose and a sassy grin, strolled around the corner. On his heels, looking like a smaller twin minus the grin appeared another boy.

The first boy introduced them. "I'm Wally McGinnis and this is my brother, Ben. We came over to see if you want your trunks carted."

I stepped forward and opened my handbag. "That would be very nice. We're strangers to your town. There appears to be only one hotel."

"Yup, my ma runs it. She keeps a clean bed and sets a good table. And she has an extry room. Two gandy dancers moved out this morning."

A gandy dancer sounded terribly heathenish, but I kept the thought to myself, thankful they had left and made room for us.

"By the looks of things, this town's kinda dead," Emmylou observed.

Wally's eyes lit up. "Ha! Ya oughta see it on Saturday nights when all the miners and tie cutters hit town. The saloons can't hold 'em all. Why, just last Saturday somebody stole ma's bloomers off the clothes line and run them up the flag pole."

He paused, then added, "Ma's a stout woman and they were as big as a bedsheet."

Ben, who'd been occupied by pushing a bare toe in and out of a knothole in the floor, uttered his first words. "Aww, Wally, they don't want to hear anymore of that. Let's get the cart and pull the trunks home."

The Prospect Hotel, whose planed boards had never known a coat of paint, stood two stories tall with a false front about midway in the line of buildings facing the railroad tracks. Double doors opened directly onto a boardwalk. It pleased me to see crisp dimity curtains and potted geraniums at the two large windows flanking the doors.

The boys led us out of the afternoon sunlight into a large central hall smelling strongly of kerosene. Turning to the left, they ushered us through a door marked, "office." I was delighted to discover the room as neat and cozy as Aunt Dolly's sitting room. Ruffled doilies, flower-festooned lamps and potted palms were liberally strewn about the pale green room.

A wizened old lady in a lace cap dozed in one of the wooden rockers lined up along the far wall. Her chair rested in the patch of sunlight streaming through the window.

Even Wally's bellowing summons to his mother failed to lift the old lady's chin from her chest. The delectable aroma of frying chicken wafted from the direction he'd aimed his voice.

A mountain of flesh waddled into the room, her felt carpet slippers slapping the groaning floor. Fat oozed from the sleeve and neck openings of the loose Mother Hubbard she wore. Wally's description of bedsheet-sized bloomers floated through my mind. This had to be Mrs. McGinnis.

She smiled pleasantly in greeting, causing her black button eyes to virtually disappear inside the folds of flesh.

"Do tell, but just happens there's a room for you ladies. Another few days and the railroad's sending in some new crews. We'll be stuffing them in every corner," she said in a husky voice as she puffed behind a tall desk set in the corner by the door.

"Do tell, but it's finding help that's got me up a crick. Your beds aren't even made up yet. Sheets still hanging on the lines."

While registering us in her big book, she cleverly drew out details about us I'd rather have kept hidden. Emmylou, with her bent for talking on one hand and her desire to remain illusive on the other, delivered a tale so full of holes that it would be impossible for us not to fall through one.

Mrs. McGinnis refrained from comment but I was sure she was nobody's fool and was forming her own opinion about the two of us.

I felt uneasy. Never having had occasion to be deceitful in my life, I hated the idea of being identified with Emmylou's tall tales. But before I could decide on a course of action, what looked like a walking clothesbasket advanced toward us.

"Do tell," Mrs. McGinnis boomed, "but here's Peggy O'Brien with your bedsheets."

The clothesbasket, overflowing with snowy sheets, dropped to the floor revealing the bearer, a young woman as small as myself, with black hair, Irish blue eyes and startlingly red cheeks.

She dropped a little curtsy and said, "Bless me, and 'tis two young ladies we be having here."

Following Mrs. McGinnis's orders, the five of us trooped out the door and into the hall. Peggy had been advised to lead us to our second floor room, while Wally and Ben were to deliver our baggage.

Peggy skittered across the hall and up the stairs in an apron so big it wrapped around her twice with room to spare. Emmylou and I had offered to carry the clothesbasket between us, to which Peggy exclaimed, "Bless you, and 'tis past believin'."

As usual, the stairs proved awkward for me. Even without the hindrance of a bulky load of sheets, stairs and my injured hip have never been compatible. No remarks were made about my staggering progress, but Peggy kept rolling her eyes toward the ceiling and muttering under her breath. I credited Wally and Ben's silence to either indifference or good manners. Only time and closer acquaintance would tell which.

While we assisted Peggy with the bedmaking, she cleared up the mystery of the strong smell of kerosene. " 'Tis Mrs. McGinnis that not be havin' a bedbug in the place. T'was her that be havin' me wash the bed with that smelly stuff. This you'll have to be rememberin', t'was gandy dancers this room just left, do you see?"

"Gandy dancers?" I questioned. "Wally mentioned something about them. It bothers me a bit that we're occupying a room just vacated by immoral women. Did they work in a saloon around here?"

Peggy stiffened in surprise. "Whist that you be askin'?"

Suddenly Emmylou flopped over the end of the bedrail, her seat upended, and howled with laughter. The two monstrous purple roses on her hat waved while she whooped and kicked.

Peggy's mouth fell into a perfect O as she gazed at this exhibition. I'm sure an encounter with an Irish leprechaun couldn't have startled her more.

I watched Emmylou's display with amazement, which quickly turned to annoyance, then anger. Marching over to the bed, I grabbed her hat, flung it across the room and pounded on her back.

"Emmylou, would you kindly stop laughing like a hyena and make some sense?"

Peering up at me through tear-filled eyes, she snorted, "I'll be blamed if you religious folks don't smell sin in everything. Honey, a gandy dancer's a gent that works on a railroad section gang."

Flabbergasted, I sank into a ladder-back chair.

Peggy took this opportunity to put the finishing touches on making the bed, grab her basket and slip out the door, muttering a few words to the ceiling as she left.

Until the dinner bell rang at six sharp, I ignored Emmylou. Whistling through the gaps in her teeth, she spent the time sorting through her box of herbs while I took refuge in writing a less-than-honest letter to Aunt Dolly. How could I shatter her confidence in me? So far, in the few days since we'd parted, I'd spent more time on my face than on my two feet. A yearning for what I had left behind overcame me and did not subside until I entered the hotel dining room with Emmylou.

She claimed a chair immediately while I hesitated in the doorway. About twenty people, mostly men in working attire, had scattered themselves around a long, cloth-covered table. Heavy white crockery lined the table's edges, leaving room in the center for milk pitchers, yellow wedges of butter and several cut-glass dishes containing jelly. The ruby-red jelly and bright green pickles added a splash of color to the stark white surroundings. Mouth-watering smells wafted from heaped platters and bowls set conveniently about the table.

Compared to the lavishly decorated dining room of the Bishop Place, the room was a poor second. But after my train journey, I rated the practical room a blessing. And the food—fit for a king.

Evidently no one stood on ceremony. I had barely laid my napkin across my lap when a blessing boomed out from the far end of the table. "Bless this food. Amen." Emmylou quickly shoved a steaming bowl of mashed potatoes under my nose. My wrist nearly snapped from the weight.

I found myself seated on the end of one side of the table. My neighbor to the right was the little lady we'd seen napping earlier. She appeared fragile, much too weak to bear the weight of the bowl. She also seemed quite dull until she raised hooded eyes and I caught a quick-witted glance. As if reading my thoughts, she said, "Never judge a book by its cover."

A man seated across the table bent forward and asked, "Now, Grandma Espie, aren't you going to introduce me to your charming friend?"

I looked up to see a man, handsome enough to be framed, smiling at me. He had attractive, even features set off by an abundance of black hair that waved back from a high forehead. A well-shaped red mustache covered his upper lip. His eyes were a rusty brown, and one of them closed in a wink, as though we shared a secret.

Flustered, I returned my attention to Grandma Espie. "May I help you with your servings?"

Instead of answering, she cleared her throat and recited in a high, sing-song voice: "Beware of that man, be he friend or brother, whose hair is one color and mustache another."

Before I could come to any conclusion about her words, the man with the red mustache and black hair threw back his head and laughed until the cutlery bounced.

Naturally this drew the attention of my fellow diners. Emmylou jabbed me in the ribs and asked, "Who's that handsome devil, Mercy?"

"I don't know," I whispered as the table's occupants returned to the business of eating. I received the impression that Mr. Red Mustache's outbursts weren't out of the ordinary.

"Well, now," he said calmly, his laughter controlled as easily as closing a door, "I'll introduce myself. I'm Ike McAnn and our table isn't often graced with two such lovely ladies."

Emmylou spoke right up. "I'm Miss Emmylou Brown and this here is Miss Mercy Bishop. We be touring the West."

For one swift moment his eyes registered astonishment. Then, a quick blink replaced the look with polite interest. "My, my, and how long will we have the pleasure of your company?"

Emmylou stuffed a jam-laden biscuit into her mouth, so I was forced to answer.

"We're uncertain at this time," I said primly.

Peggy, who had spent the meal traveling between the table and the kitchen, arrived with an enormous, gray enameled pot of coffee.

While she filled Emmylou's cup, Emmylou dismayed me by asking pointed questions about the hotel laundry. Was there no end to her lack of refinement, I fumed. Discussing dirty linens at the table with the hired girl!

Mentally dismissing Emmylou and Mr. McAnn, I gave my attention to the best meal I'd eaten since my farewell dinner at Aunt Dolly's.

Refusing to be ignored, however, Mr. McAnn drew Emmylou into conversation by asking her with which hand she stirred her coffee.

Emmylou smiled broadly. "My left. Any doctor worth her salt favors her left hand."

Primed and waiting, Mr. McAnn spit back, "I use a spoon myself."

Chuckling behind his napkin, his rust-brown eyes found mine and seemed to ask, "What do you think of me?"

Elbowing the man to his right, he asked, "Say, Hoss, did you hear that? This lovely lady's a doctor. Just what you need."

Hoss was the most peculiar looking individual. He honestly resembled a horse. The lines in his face, a long nose with a drip on the end, shaggy brows and blubbery lips all plunged downward toward a long chin where a few "horse whiskers" bristled. Being as bald as an egg increased the appearance of length to his face. His small and wide-set eyes peered at Emmylou from beneath long, stiff lashes.

When he spoke in a horse-like whinny, I nearly

61

choked on a bite of chicken. "Hoofnagle, George Hoofnagle be my handle. And it ain't a secret, I'm puny and ready to die on the vine."

"Really." Emmylou excitedly leaned into her dinner plate. "You need a swig of my herb tea. Did ya ever douse yer vitals with honeysuckle or mullein or with a snitch of tansy? That'll put ya in fine fettle."

"Our friend here," Mr. McAnn interrupted with a smirk, "relies heavily on Dr. Leeson's Tiger Oil."

As if by signal, Hoss dug under the red cloth wound around his neck and pulled out a flat brown bottle. Using his teeth, long and stained like a horse's, he yanked the cork out, tossed some of the bottle's contents into the back of his throat and wiped his full lips with the cuff of his shirt.

Fascinated, I watched this ritual until Mr. McAnn caught my attention and boldly winked.

An apple pie being passed around saved me from analyzing why my cheeks felt warm and my palms moist. I focused on the spicy, tart fruit and flaky crust of my pie.

The meal quickly came to a close with the finishing of dessert. Appetites satiated, the diners left the crowded room in pairs or singles, presumably to smoke on the big side porch or stroll about town. Furtively studying the men as they brushed past my chair, I guessed some of them would end up in one of the several saloons lined up along Prospect's lone street.

So intent was I on my examination of the unknown men at the table that I failed to see when Hoss and Mr. McAnn departed. Even Emmylou took off without a word. A small girl in pigtails took Grandma Espie off to bed. How much of the table conversation she'd absorbed I didn't know, but she had laid bony fingers on my hand and murmured, "Handsome is as handsome does."

After brushing the last crumbs from my lips, my goal for the evening was to enjoy a period of quiet reflection in my room. I lifted my skirts and hurried through the parlor-like office only to find the door barricaded by a man with an assortment of children while a woman banged on the service bell for attention.

I'd no sooner edged behind one of the rockers, waiting for an opportune moment to slip out the door, when a fat little boy with wet pants crawled across my feet on his way to a potted fern. Just before he dropped a handful of dirt on my toe, Mrs. McGinnis shuffled into the room.

Flipping the tail of her apron in the air, she puffed, "Do tell if it ain't our mayor's wife. Mrs. Skillings, what are you doing here?"

The bellringer stepped forward, a thickset, well corseted woman with a back as stiff as a ramrod. "Yes, Mrs. McGinnis, I've brought the Reverend Rube Golden. He's an old friend who's just come in on The Local. It is my esteemed honor to welcome him to this benighted locality where he's heard the call to spread the glorious Gospel of Light to the heathen."

Pausing for breath, she turned to the Reverend Rube Golden and clutching his elbow, propelled him forward for an introduction. "Reverend Golden, I'd like you to meet Mrs. McGinnis. She will be one of your most faithful parishioners, I know."

Reverend Golden was a tall, thin man with grey creeping into his sandy hair. He acknowledged the introduction with a slight nod and a pleasant smile.

He appeared tired and anticipatory at the same time as he gestured around the room. "These are my children. I'm looking forward to bringing the gospel to you all."

The Reverend's brood of youngsters, mostly preschool age it appeared, were no doubt travel-worn and thus acted like children on the last day of school. He surveyed their antics a moment, then said with a hint of apology for their behavior, "Their mother has recently gone on to be with the Lord."

Reverend Golden continued, "Another friend of mine from Missouri, Mr. Levi Miller, was to make arrangements for us. Could you be so kind as to direct us to him?"

Levi Miller!

Just beyond the preacher I suddenly spied a young lady half-hidden by the coat rack. She looked for all the world like a glass madonna, an ornament, I decided just as one of the children mashed my toe beneath the rocker of the chair she'd whipped into a wild gallop.

Ignoring my smarting toe, I spun about at Mrs. Skillings' next words. "Yes, the Reverend Golden came at the pleading of the mayor, myself and Levi Miller. We all resided in the same town back in Missouri. When Mrs. Golden departed this life for her reward in heavenly mansions, we felt he needed a change of scenery and no one can argue but what this godless country needs him."

I gasped! I'd nearly come to the conclusion that Levi Miller didn't exist. I was all ears, listening to Mrs. McGinnis's next words.

"So you're Levi's friend. W'all that man don't make it into town much with nothing but a mule

64

track between here and Bear Canyon, but he's always a sight for sore eyes. He were in just the day afore yesterday with another one of them cats for my Sally. You're to live atop what was that big store building three doors west. Ain't much finished inside, but you can thank your lucky stars to find any kind of cover in this town. I ain't got a room to give you. I'm filled up to the attic."

Mrs. Skillings' glasses quivered. "While a minister of the gospel must be prepared to make sacrifices for his Lord, we thank God, not the stars He created, Mrs. McGinnis. It appears to me that we are getting a minister none too soon."

During this exchange the Reverend Golden teetered on his heels and studied the ceiling, an amused twinkle in his eyes.

"Thank you, Mrs. McGinnis," Reverend Golden said graciously. "It will do just fine. Is there someone to help us with our baggage? I have about all I can handle with the children," he apologized again.

"My younguns can help you and there's always fellers hanging around with time on their hands. I'll round them up on my way back to the kitchen."

Taking this as my exit cue, I scampered up to our room. Once inside I was drawn to the window and the pastel lights filling the sky. Pink streaks darted out from the tall mountain peaks hiding the setting sun. Those sharp peaks guarded the little valley where Prospect huddled. They also stood sentinel over access to the rest of the world, reminding me that the only way of escape was that toy train that snaked over precarious rails.

Movement on the street below drew my eyes from the mountains. The Golden tribe, led by the

Reverend and Mrs. Skillings filed across the dusty street, skirting the waist-high tree stumps, to the depot. The children jumped about like popcorn in a hot skillet while Miss Madonna drifted behind. My sympathies were with the preacher. He seemed a good man but almost overwhelmed by his new tasks of being sole parent to his children while at the same time evangelizing a new community.

I decided I wouldn't tell Emmylou about Levi Miller's interest in bringing a preacher to Prospect. I could just imagine what she'd have to say about that! Men were such a confusing lot!

The doorknob banged against the wall as Emmylou bounded in and flopped in a chair driving all thoughts of men and silent madonnas from my mind.

"Mercy," she panted, "ya gotta hand it to me. I've landed a job so's we can keep body and soul together."

"Really?"

"Yup, I'm gonna do all the hotel washin' in that little log shack that sets alongside the hotel. Me and you can live in it. Gertie McGinnis be plumb tickled to get somebody to do up her washin'."

I moved over to the bed and sat on the edge. I groped for the right words but none came to mind. Finally I offered weakly, "I'll help you all I can."

Sounding skeptical, Emmylou said, "Mercy, now ya look me in the eye. Have ya ever wrung out a wet bed sheet?"

I studied my slim fingers silently before obeying her command to look her in the eye. I had to settle for the left one for a greasy strand of hair covered the right one. I met her steady gaze without answering.

66

"Don't ya worry none." Emmylou read the answer in my eyes. "We'uns will have to land on something else for ya to do," she said simply.

I couldn't help smiling at my champion. She might be an untidy murderess but she had solved our immediate need while I, a proper young lady, vacillated in genteel confusion.

Chapter 5

As Emmylou and I left the hotel the next morning, I shivered beneath my heavy wool shawl. At this early hour the sun still hadn't evicted Jack Frost from the valley floor.

"Emmylou, this cabin we're going to move into is snug, isn't it?" I asked.

White vaporous puffs accompanied Emmylou's words. "Far as I could make out. 'Course it were some dark when I looked at it after supper last night. It do have a right good stove but the wood stack appeared mighty piddlin'."

"What can we do about it?" I worried. "Here it is only September and there's frost already. And I do wish you'd accepted the loan of a coat."

Emmylou still wore her traveling costume, now firmly buttoned. A button in my sewing box had been a near match.

"Honey," Emmylou explained as if talking to a dullard, "the woods are full of wood. And there appears to be men fallin' all over theirselves to help us. We play our cards right and afore ya can flutter your eyes at 'em, they'll be fightin' over who gets to rescue the maidens in distress."

The cabin, whose dimensions closely resembled those of my bedroom at the Bishop Place, looked like a wart attached to the two story hotel. A light push failed to dislodge the door. It wasn't until Emmylou rammed her shoulder against the rough planks that it gave a protesting shudder and grated far enough across the floor for us to gain access. All my senses rebelled against following Emmylou through that dim opening. The stale, cold air that assailed my nostrils reminded me of an old cellar overladen with repugnant odors.

Emmylou's head appeared around the door jamb. "Mercy, stop wrinkling your nose and get in here," she ordered. "Ain't ya ever smelled rats afore? Yup, rats," she repeated at my dismayed expression. "They stake out their territory with the call of nature trick."

My hand flew to my mouth. "Oh, Emmylou," I shuddered. "Do we *have* to live in such a vile place?"

Emmylou squeezed through the door opening and shook her head until several strands of straw-colored hair fell from their pins.

"And pray tell, Miss High and Mighty, where do you make out we go? Gertie told me plain that she needs that room for some fellers comin' in to work on the railroad. She plans to jam more beds in and git them men under cover by nightfall. And we ain't got the money to stay there more than a night or two, nohow."

Chagrined, I gulped and meekly allowed Emmylou to pull me into our future home. Thankfully, the two tiny, dust-filmed windows shed a minimum of light on the room's condition.

As if in a trance, I limped after Emmylou, only to be brought to reality when I became enmeshed in a cobweb.

"Help!" I screamed, while vainly clawing at the sticky substance.

Indifferent to such a trifling annoyance, Emmylou shoved a broom in my face and told me to roll up my sleeves and get to work.

The business of purging that little room of soot, rodent droppings, overly active insect life and other unidentifiable filth began. And it continued without ceasing throughout the day until twenty or so mop buckets later my hip screamed, "I quit!" And I crumpled alongside my string mop.

Before I could move, Emmylou grabbed me under the arms and dragged me to the corner which housed the rusty iron bed. There she dumped me on the dingy straw tick.

"I'll get ya something," she muttered, just as a breathtaking pain pierced through my body.

The brew Emmylou dribbled into my mouth put some fire into me.

"Ugh," I sputtered, and pushed the cup away from my lips. "That burns all the way down."

"Nothing to git all fired up about. Put a little starch in your backbone."

I pushed myself to a sitting position, sagging against the metal rails of the bed. Emmylou hovered over me, armed with her still full cup. She looked like the end of a hard winter. A sooty line ran down one cheek. Her hair, resembling a haystack attacked by hungry cattle, tumbled into the grubby collar of her shirtwaist which gaped open again, this time right below the bustline.

Evidently she wasn't favorably impressed with me, either. "Ya better have another swig. Ya don't look none too pert."

Obediently I took another sip of the fiery liquid and promptly choked.

With tears streaming down my cheeks, I sputtered, "Emmylou, that isn't ardent spirits, is it? I do not believe in drinking intoxicating beverages."

Emmylou rose, patted my clenched fists and grinned. "Doctor's secret. Do ya feel up to supper? There's the bell now."

In my astonishment at her suggestion, I nearly missed the clanging tones of the large dinner bell anchored to the hotel's side porch.

"Emmylou, how can you consider appearing at a table? Just look at us." I shuddered with horror. Obeying my own command, I gazed at my dirt-streaked skirt. And my hands! One day's labor had turned them into cracked, bleeding eyesores with every nail torn to filthy, jagged shreds.

"Well," Emmylou answered, while making some wild jabs at her hair. "I worked like a slavey today and I'm hungry. Meals come with my job and I aim to eat."

Tenderly easing toward the edge of the straw tick, I pointed toward my trunks which Wally and Ben had delivered earlier.

"Emmylou, at least accept the loan of a clean shirtwaist. I don't think my skirts will fit around you."

Emmylou had submerged her face in a water bucket, thus preventing an immediate answer. Sputtering up out of the water, she said, "Honey, your waists ain't gonna fit me no better. Me as big as a cow and you as flat as a ironin' board. But I'll wrap that shawl of yours around me."

After Emmylou's departure, I dragged myself across the floor and appropriated hot water from the kettles on the stove for my bath. This completed, I slipped into a ribbon-trimmed housecoat and perched on the edge of the bed, evaluating my new home now that it was clean.

Rough log walls and splintery floors, minus one splinter which felt like a barbed hook beneath my thumbnail, enclosed me. The furnishings consisted of a woodstove, a wooden crate nailed to the wall for a cabinet, and the sagging bed upon which I rested. The smell of damp wood and lye soap now permeated everything. *Bare.* I sighed as I curled into a ball on the bed and drifted off to sleep.

Emmylou's return from supper lifted me from a deep slumber.

"Hey, Mercy, lookee what I brung us! Blankets, pillows, and such."

Peering from beneath still-heavy lids, I became aware that Emmylou was pushing the door open with her hip while her arms were piled high with bedding. She wedged her way through the slight opening, then a heavy boot behind her forced the door wide.

The boot disappeared and Ike McAnn backed into view. He supported one end of a wooden table and Hoss bore the other. They plopped the table in the middle of the room. Ike surveyed the room with sharp eyes while Hoss wiped his dripping nose with his shirt sleeve.

Although both men were of medium size, they seemed to crowd our little house. Modestly, I cowered behind the stack of bedding Emmylou had dumped on the bed just as Ike's roving inspection came across me.

"Good evening, Miss Bishop. I'm sorry to hear that you're under the weather."

I dragged the top blanket over me while Ike grinned. He elbowed Hoss and nodded his handsome head in my direction. "Miss Bishop here's so shy she'd go into the closet to change her mind."

Then, hands in his pockets, he rocked back on his heels and chortled at his own joke.

Speechless, I continued to peek at this puzzling man over the edge of the blanket. I noticed his humor didn't reach his eyes.

Emmylou broke a momentary silence. "Mercy, your green eyes are popping out. I jest knew you'd be plumb tickled about the table and all." She paused and looked in the direction of the doorway. "And here are Wally and Ben with the chairs. Their ma's gonna loan them to us to make room for more beds in the hotel."

She clapped her hands in glee before continuing. "We're a-gonna be as cozy as a couple of cats in a hayloft. Ike, you and George set yourselves down."

Before they could obey, Peggy breezed in with a towel-covered tray. She squeezed through the crowd to the bed and curtsied. "Bless you and all, Miss Bishop. Mrs. McGinnis is sending your supper."

She placed the tray on the table and whirled toward the door. Ike's fingers encircled her thin wrist, arresting her flight. He winked at her and asked, "And how's our little Irish colleen this evening?"

Quivering like a frightened rabbit, she broke from his grip and scampered into the dusk.

Still clutching the blanket beneath my chin, I breathed a sigh of relief when the four males refused Emmylou's hospitality and left us to the privacy of our new home.

The venison stew, hot tea, and cornbread soothed my hunger pains and revived me enough to assist Emmylou with the bedmaking. Before we began she lit a kerosene lamp and its soft glow made our humble cabin appear almost homey.

"I got some news that ought to do your heart good," Emmylou said as we tucked in sheets and blankets.

"There's a preacher that's moved to town and they's having a preachin' tomorrow morning at eleven in that big store building three doors down. Gertie bellered it out at the supper table tonight. I'm gonna help Peggy git dinner on tomorrow noon so's Gertie can go to the preachin'. As religious as ya be, I know'd you'd be as happy as a clam."

Emmylou's wide smile revealed the joy she felt in bringing me this information.

How could someone so good-hearted irritate me so often? I wondered. But I didn't spoil her pleasure at her announcement.

When she described herself as "wrung to a frazzle," Emmylou spoke for both of us and we prepared for bed.

After the lamp was blown out to insure privacy from anyone passing our uncovered windows, the last light of day shown through the western window and fell into a four-piece patch on our scrubbed floor. Sinking into bed we rustled about until we found spots with a minimum of lumps.

I think I could sleep on a bed of nails, I mused. Just as blessed sleep quietly enveloped me, Emmylou hissed in my ear, "Mercy!"

I refused to open my eyes.

"Mercy," she persisted.

Nestling further into the straw tick, I murmured resignedly, "Yes?"

"Mercy, I think that Ike's got his eye on ya. And I smell trouble."

Sleep fled. And for reasons unknown to me, I came to his defenses with a splutter. "What do you know about him?"

"He's a man, honey, and men's one critter I knows about."

I had no answer to that, so turning on my side I drew the covers over my head and prayed that God would enlighten *me* concerning men. Since they were half of His creation, He ought to know about their habits and I had a gnawing suspicion that I would need some of that knowledge before too many days passed.

The next morning I hummed, "What A Friend We Have In Jesus," while preparing for church. It lifted my spirits so much that I momentarily overlooked the inconveniences of residing in a crude log cabin in Prospect, Montana.

As I pulled on my chemise, stepped into my petticoats, and wiggled into my skirt, lingering pain from my hip dampened my spirits somewhat. My song faltered even more as I tried to arrange my thick hair into its bun using only a small, cracked hand mirror.

Emmylou had improvised an ironing board, using a plank and the backs of our two chairs. Lifting the heavy irons from the stove to press wrinkles from my tucked lawn waist, the inconveniences refused to be ignored any longer. My song faded completely.

Strangely silent, Emmylou had kept a fire roaring and prepared tea and toast. Sitting at the table, she drummed her fingers on its top and watched me as I finished off my costume with a matching bolero jacket boasting fashionable leg-of-mutton sleeves. It was generously trimmed in dark blue velvet.

I'd considered using the curling iron on the hair framing my face, but gave it up in the next thought and gently lifted a gorgeous hat from its protective nest in one of my trunks. I'd purchased it from a local milliner just before I'd left Oak Grove. Fashioned in the latest style, it was flat and had a short brim piled high with ribbons, netting and blue violets to match my suit. After I had anchored it with a long hat pin, I longed for a good mirror but assured myself that under the primitive conditions I'd do.

My pleasure at appearing fashionable was dashed when Emmylou spoke. "Ya'all say a prayer for me. I guess I'd kinda like to go to the preaching, but, dog my cats a body's gotta own a lot of trappin's to go to church. No wonder I ain't never had an invite."

I looked up while pulling a glove over a work-mutilated hand. "Emmylou, you have the wrong idea. People go to church to worship God. And God looks on the heart, not the outward appearance. You'd be more than welcome. I thought you weren't interested."

"That so." Emmylou said drily as she crumpled the tail of the apron she wore. The brevity of her answer spoke volumes and gave me much to mull over as we left our log home. I'd make her a new dress, I resolved. If anyone needed one, she did.

Emmylou and I parted at the hotel steps. I hurried down the street, inhaling the invigorating mountain air. After awhile, the picture of the sun shining on pristine mountain peaks chased away nagging worries. Miss Mercy Bishop, late of Oak Grove, Iowa, began a Sunday morning.

No one joined me as I traveled over the hotel boardwalk, down to a packed dirt path, beyond an overgrown vacant lot and past a small board building that had a row of gold letters painted on its window. I paused to read:

Oscar Skillings—Editor, "Weekly Prospect"
                    Mayor • Sheriff • Recorder
                              et alii

If I recalled my Latin, that meant and so forth. Hmmm.

I passed one more structure, then came to a square, two story building I presumed to be the church.

The door stood open to the morning sun. Leaving its brightness behind, I entered a cavernous room. As my eyes adjusted to the change of light, I saw a number of people darting back and forth. I couldn't control my first thought: Was Levi Miller one of them? The answer wasn't immediate, but I did recognize the Golden children. Wally and Ben McGinnis, along with three others, shoved an odd assortment of chairs and benches about while Gertie McGinnis barked orders from her seat in the back row.

As I continued to stand at the door surveying the scene, Mrs. Skillings propelled Reverend Golden

78

away from the kitchen table pulpit and into a corner. Imperiously motioning to someone, a man I had not yet met joined their whispered consultation.

A frazzled-looking woman hurried up to the trio.

"Mrs. Skillings, Mrs. Skillings, you are going to present the new preacher, aren't you? You bein' the mayor's wife, and all, I think it only proper that you offer the introductions."

The thickset, well-corseted woman straightened her already ramrod posture, looked through glasses perched precariously on a hook nose, and announced, "Oh, of course, my dear. Who else should present the new parson?"

Obviously not expecting an answer she hurried over to a young woman who stood beside me in the doorway. As Mrs. Skillings greeted the woman, I turned and saw the young lady I had seen briefly at the hotel. Her skin was pale and flawless. I had never seen such cool serenity on the face of one so young.

I moved out of the doorway and realized there were few others in the room. I wondered if anyone else besides Grandma Espie, who sat beside Mrs. McGinnis, her portly daughter, would attend church. Maybe the news hadn't gotten around.

That question was answered as others, making elongated shadows in the sunny doorway, entered the building. Mrs. Skillings sailed around the room possessively, urging everyone to find a seat. Services would begin soon.

I settled into the back row. The seats filled quickly and quietly. The novelty of the situation seemed to place a constraint on the group. A middle-aged couple took the two chairs directly in front of me. Soon three men edged their way across the couple's toes to occupy the rest of the seats in that row. I recognized Ike, handsome in a gray worsted suit, and smelled Hoss. Onion, or maybe garlic.

Just before Preacher Golden cleared his throat for attention, little Sally McGinnis squeezed in beside me. "How do you like my ribbons?" she whispered, flipping the ends of her pigtails in my face. A red ribbon adorned each.

I hugged her close, thinking of Tibby James, and assured her, "I think they're lovely."

She nestled into the crook of my arm and I focused my attention on Mrs. Skillings who was about to speak.

"We are very pleased to welcome all of you to the first church services in Prospect, Montana." She seemed to swell with self-importance.

"We have our kind neighbor, Levi Miller, to thank for arranging this meeting and lending us the use of his building. Come up here, Levi, and direct us in some singing," Mrs. Skillings finished.

Sally almost landed on the floor as I slid to the edge of my chair to peek between the couple seated in front of me. But the upheaval was unnecessary because Levi Miller proved to be of such height that even a shorty like me on the back row couldn't miss him.

Tall and lean, he studied the book that rested on his long fingers and stammered, "L-l-let's sing, 'When I Survey The Wondrous Cross.' "

Mrs. Skillings, stationed at his side, played a chord on an accordion strapped across her front. Levi Miller raised a hand to signal the beginning of the song. His rich baritone led us through the verses of that majestic hymn. Except for one quick glance, he kept his eyes on the hymnal so I felt free to stare rudely. His brown, short-cropped hair, obviously plastered down, rebelliously bristled up at the crown giving him a little boy look. His protruding ears and knobby wrists which were exposed by the too-short sleeves of his navy suit added to the impression of a youngster in the midst of a growing spurt.

Maternally, I determined to protect him from Emmylou's onslaught. Then in the next second I chided myself. How ridiculous! I knew nothing about him and after the trick he'd played on us, he needed reprimanding.

Between Scripture readings, he led in two more hymns. His singing voice was sure and true, but when he read he appeared slow and hesitant. Perhaps a guilty conscience hampered spontaneity, I reasoned critically.

Standing behind the makeshift pulpit, Preacher Golden seemed to possess more inner strength and integrity than my first impression had allowed. He held the Bible open in his hand and authoritatively preached from Philippians 4:11: "Not that I speak in respect of want: for I have learned, in whatsoever state I am, therewith to be content." The Reverend's knowledgeable exposition of the verse was impressive, and the Holy Spirit used those words of the Apostle Paul to shame me. I confessed myself lacking and silently prayed that I would learn contentment living in a log shack with Emmylou, and even in facing the bleak, uncertain future forced upon me by Elmer Swindley and perpetuated by Levi Miller.

Within minutes of Preacher Golden's closing

"Amen," his hymn choice of "Blest Be The Tie That Binds" drew us together with hearty handshakes, slaps on the back, and formal introductions.

In warm confusion, I met Hank and Hattie Loftus who owned Prospect's General Emporium, and Oscar Skillings, mayor and editor of the "Weekly Prospect," who had a careworn, old man called Bigfoot in tow. Before I could examine his feet, Gertie McGinnis stood before me with three woodcutters.

With muscles bulging under their plaid shirts, they looked strong enough to sling logs but their kind faces made me suspect they'd tiptoe around a woodland flower. Before I could conclude whether Jack was the one wearing blue plaid and no whiskers, or whether Mike had the big nose and red plaid, or Otto sported suspenders, Ike appeared.

With a firm grip on my elbow he walked me out the door and over to the hotel dining room. Hoss trailed along behind, hacking and spitting until I feared for the hem of my skirt.

Naturally, Ike apropriated the chair next to mine and I spent the meal a-tremble. When his mustache brushed my forehead as he leaned down to tell me how adorable I looked, my cheeks burned. And when those same red hairs tickled my ear while he confidently whispered that gazing at me made him forget his eternal vow to bachelorhood, I clasped my hands over my heart, positive that organ had stopped beating.

Still lightheaded, I nearly missed his next comment. But words that sounded like *Levi Miller* restored my sanity. "I'm sorry, but did you say something about Levi Miller?"

He studied my face. "Yeah, what'd you think of

that Levi Miller who directed the hymn singing?"

Since he'd been so recently on my mind, I answered without hesitation. "He seemed painfully shy."

A tiny smile played at the corners of Ike's mouth, causing his mustache to quiver. "That man ain't afraid of anything he can wrestle or shoot. He'd take on a bear or an ugly man or protect some little critter like a young'un or a cat—cats he's crazy about—and old ladies don't scare him none. But any unattached female reduces him to a blathering idiot," Ike said contemptuously.

"You seem to know him well," I said in surprise.

Ike shrugged. "I've had my dealings with him."

"Do you think he's capable of duplicity?"

"Of what?"

"Of being less than honest," I explained.

"Oh sure, and just between you and me I'm sure he's trying to get a woman for his ranch. He wants some young'uns of his own but he'd never have the guts, excuse me, nerve to court a woman proper-like."

Before we could continue this most informative conversation, a burly man with a voice like a Jersey bull cut in. "Hey, Ike, stop hogging the beautiful ladies and give us all a chance."

With this crude remark, our table companions, whom I noticed for the first time were all male with the exception of Grandma Espie at the far end, looked our way.

"Ya shoulda brought her down to the Watering Hole last night," another man said. He grinned around a mouthful of food and winked at me with a bloodshot eye.

Mortified, I shoved the last bite in my mouth and excused myself to Ike, saying I was going to the kitchen to help Emmylou with the dishes.

As I turned the white china knob, someone remarked, "Say, Ike, remember that gal with the pink parasol?" I quickly shut the door on their burst of laughter.

Once inside the kitchen, my confusion expanded to include the scene being enacted in the corner beside the oversized black range. Levi Miller sat upon a chair, with Emmylou and Sally on either side of him, earnestly attending a calico cat stretched across his bony knees.

"Hold her mouth open, Levi," Emmylou was saying as calmly as though she hadn't just yesterday declared war on him. And wasn't this the man who quaked in his boots when around young females?

"That potion ought to cure or kill her," Gertie chuckled. Stuffed into a rocker, her feet resting on the open oven door, she watched the doctoring.

This brought an immediate protest from Sally. Rushing over to Gertie, she pounded on her mother's fleshy arm. "Mama, don't say that! Emmylou's a doctor and she's gonna get Cat back on her feet."

Having finished with her patient, Emmylou straightened up and acknowledged me. "Howdy, Mercy."

Levi Miller gently stroked the cat, ignoring us humans.

"That were just dandelion roots and mullein leaves smashed in goose oil. Ain't a better tonic around," Emmylou explained to the little girl.

Pacified, Sally returned to the corner and, leaning

against Levi's long leg, assisted him in cheering the patient.

At that moment Peggy flew through the door with a pile of plates and cheeks the color of cherries. She nearly knocked me off my feet. "Bless you and all, Miss Bishop, I'm sorry. But those men do aggravate me, they do."

Especially Ike, with his good looks and sweet words, I guessed grimly.

The dishes clattered onto a drainboard. Peggy tended to the water steaming in pots on the stove, industrious as a bee. Gertie picked up a plate and fanned her face with it just as Emmylou ordered me to the corner to meet Levi Miller.

She shoved me within inches of his knees and said, "Mercy, I'd like you to meet Levi Miller."

I studied her face for some clue to her unexpected behavior and, finding none, I politely told the top of his head, "Pleased to meet you."

Levi Miller raised his head shyly, blue eyes filled with anxiety. "Happy to meet you, Miss Bishop."

Emmylou looked as pleased as if she'd introduced me to the King of England. "I know'd you two would be good friends," she purred.

Shaking my head slightly, I stepped back and dropped onto the bench beside the kitchen table with question chasing question around my poor aching head. Didn't he recognize my name? And why was Emmylou so pleasant to him? Had I misjudged Emmylou? Or could a woman who'd recently shot a husband, plan to stab Levi Miller in the back? Was this the man who was so anxious to obtain a wife? Had he settled on Emmylou?

Chapter 6

Emmylou wasted no time informing me why she'd changed her attitude toward Levi Miller. After the hotel dishes were finished we carried the dirty laundry to our cabin in preparation for the next day's wash.

While Emmylou shaved a bar of soap into a pan, she told me, "That thar man be as innocent as a new hatched egg. He'd drown a cat afore he'd go writin' letters fer a wife. Women make him nervous nohow."

"He didn't seem that shy with you," I countered, while the sharp smell of lye soap pinched my nostrils.

"That's cause I never gave him a chance. I told ya, I knows men."

She brushed her hands together to dust off soap crumbs and went to our box shelf. "Now, I gotta jar of mutton tallow here and I want ya to rub it in your hands. I'm thinkin' ya can hang out sheets termorrow if I fetch them out to the lines fer ya."

Skirting the piles of dirty laundry, I took the hand cream and applied it to my chapped hands. The creamy substance did much to relieve the dry soreness.

But my mind found no relief in Emmylou's opinions. "Who *did* write those letters then?"

Emmylou paused at the door, an empty pail in each hand. She'd told me she intended to fill all the tubs tonight in preparation for an early start in the morning.

"That thar's what I aim to nose out. I've got my suspects." Then changing the subject she said, "Now I'll wager luggin' water on Sunday be agin your religion."

I nearly answered yes before I caught myself. I had been raised believing only necessary labor should be performed on Sunday. But the idea of my sitting like a pampered lady while Emmylou struggled in with innumerable buckets of water from the pump out back didn't set well with me. I tossed the life-long rule aside and grabbed a bucket. I knew one would be all I could handle.

While I followed Emmylou out into the gathering dusk she shrugged her broad shoulders and said, " 'Spects carryin' a few buckets of water won't keep 'em from unlocking the pearly gates fer ya."

By the time I'd finished my daily Scripture reading and personal grooming the next morning, the base of our stove glowed red with heat. Vapor from the steaming kettles lined up across its top had fogged up the window panes and promised soggy living quarters before all the laundry was pinned to the lines.

True to her word, Emmylou carried the sheets, towels, tablecloths, and pillowslips outside for me to pin to the clotheslines.

As I hung the clothes on the lines, intermittent thoughts on who could have written those letters crossed my mind as I marvelled at how diligently Emmylou had labored over each piece, not once but three times. First, she'd plunge each article into a tub of boiling water, swish it about, then pull it out with a long wooden stick. Next, she'd drop the steaming piece into a sudsy tub where she'd energetically scrub it across the corrugated surface of the washboard. After a thorough wringing, the article was subjected to the rinse tub. Since Gertie possessed a wringer contraption, Emmylou didn't have to wring the water out with a strong-armed twist. Nevertheless, I was amazed at the strength of her sturdy body. Doing hotel laundry wasn't for the puny, I decided. How Peggy had managed, I couldn't guess.

Until various citizens of Prospect invaded the backyard, I delighted in my occupation. A light fall breeze fluttered the sheets after I pinned them. Gertie's chickens fussily scratched beside the hotel, while the hotel's milk source watched me with friendly brown eyes from beyond a pole fence. Only an occasional squawk from a flighty chicken shattered the peace, and it added to the pastoral setting.

As long as I didn't glance upward at the ring of peaks stretching toward the heavens, I could pretend I was back home in an Iowa farmyard with the road leading to Oak Grove running past the front gate.

Before this daydream had time to grow, I was

upended by a large hound dog. He bounded through the backyard with his tongue lolling out the side of his sagging jaw. Before I could sidestep him, he swerved and planted his front paws on my apron bib, knocking me off-balance into the laundry basket. Since the basket was nearly empty I landed in the bottom of it, clawing the air like a turtle on its back.

Then to add horror to insult, I heard a horse! Not only did it make those blubbering, snorting noises that invariably sent my heart knocking against my ribs, but it was near enough for my nose to catch that horrible scent peculiar to horses.

I was as helpless as when I'd been trapped inside a stall with Father's stallion at the age of two. The last twenty-one years had been spent carefully avoiding those big-boned creatures only to find myself about to be trampled upon in a clothes-basket. The thought drove me to rock the basket frantically.

A moist, feathery muzzle brushed my forehead. I collapsed, screaming hysterically.

Through my screams I heard the sound of Ike's riotous laughter. It didn't soften until he'd seated me on a stump. Then, he stopped laughing long enough to reason with me.

"For crying out loud, Mercy, don't take on so. Cooney and Bob just have good taste. They wanted to kiss a pretty lady while they had the chance. Can't say I blame them." His face was so close I could see the shadow of tomorrow's beard on his chin.

I hugged myself, clenching my teeth lest they begin to chatter. Peeking over Ike's shoulder I saw the object of my fears. Ike's big bay was placidly cropping the grass around a clothesline pole while

Cooney flopped at my feet.

Ike nudged my chin with his finger but I dropped my gaze to my clasped hands unable to respond to his solicitude.

Impatiently he stepped back and said, "Mercy, if you're just gonna sit there like a dunce, I got better things to do with my time." And picking up Bob's reins, he hoisted himself into the saddle, whistled at Cooney, and left me slouching on the stump.

Within minutes after Ike's departure, Gertie came outside with a pan of chicken scraps propped on the ledge of her stomach.

"Do tell, Mercy," she bellowed as soon as she saw me. "Did the clothes hanging get too much for you? You look plumb frazzled."

With me unable to manage one horse, one dog, and one male, Gertie's suggestion seemed very likely.

In answer, however, I shook my head. Stuffing my flyaway hair back into its bun, I tested my legs. Surprisingly, they not only held me upright, but conveyed me to the basket with no more than my usual limp.

Apparently thinking all was well, Gertie leaned against a clothesline pole after flinging scraps in the general direction of the chickens. Above the frenzied squawking this act put into motion, she said sociably, "You gals are lifesavers. Peggy were a godsend, but she don't weigh a hundred pounds with a rock in each pocket and some of her furren ways get on a body's nerves. But I gotta hand it to her, she isn't a-feared to work. With Ma going downhill 'til she's nothing but a shadow of her old self and my feet a-going to pieces, I need all the help I can get."

She shifted her weight from one slippered foot to the other and flicked a fly off of a tea towel before continuing. "Do tell, but I'd give a lot to know where that Wally vamoosed to. That boy can disappear faster than snow in July when there's work to be done. I told him to cut and stack some wood."

Just then the object of her complaint sprinted into sight. Tearing around the corner of our log abode, arms and legs pumping, freckles standing out on a face cut in two by an ear-to-ear grin, Wally fled behind the barn.

Before Gertie could exclaim, "Do tell," Hoss danced around the same corner. Flinging his head about, he spotted Gertie and me, then ran over to where we stood amidst the white wash.

"Which way'd that little scoundrel go?" he asked with a wild-eyed gasp.

Gertie clutched his shoulder with a pudgy hand. "Settle yourself down, Hoss. You'll never in all the world catch him. Now tell me, what's the little rascal done now?"

"He poured some cayenne pepper into my bottle of Dr. Leeson's Tiger Oil. I asked him to hold it while I was taken with a sneezing fit. When I threw that tonic down my throat it all but fried my gizzard," he whimpered.

Gertie patted his shoulder. "Do tell, I doubt you're past hope. But somebody's got to put the fear of God in that young'un or he's bound for a life of crime, certain. Only mortal that could tame him was his pa and that man, God rest his soul, has been gone these past three years."

Hoss started to sputter but Gertie ignored him. "What he needs in the worst way is some learning. That'd not give him time for all his orneriness. I've always been a great one for learning. There must be a dozen young'uns here abouts not counting the new preacher's family, and no school whatsoever.

Gertie's discourse was interrupted by the appearance of Emmylou and a packing box overflowing with laundry.

"Gertie, your prayers be answered!" Emmylou exclaimed, as she dropped the box and pointed at me. "Mercy here has learning pourin' out her ears."

"Me?" I asked in surprise. "I've never taught anyone but infants their Bible lessons and older children the piano. I wouldn't know where to begin planning a course of study in arithmetic, reading, geography and such."

Gertie grinned until her eyes became mere slits. "Do tell, but this be manna from heaven. You even sound like a schoolmarm. For my part, you can have free room and board. I'm sure the others can rake up a payment of some sort. With the railroad work, most everybody's got a couple of nickels to rub together."

Flabbergasted, I stood still while they planned.

"And honey," Emmylou told me, "with ya being a member in good standin', I bet ya can git the use of that church building fer a school room."

Gertie nearly bounced off the ground. "That's for sure. After I get the potato peeling done and after dinner is over, I'll just step over and have a little chat with the Reverend."

Emmylou nearly stepped on Hoss as she whirled about to return to her washing. Then stopping, she looked into his long face and gently guided him back to the cabin with the promise of a restorative cure.

Left alone once more with the chickens and the cow, I jabbed wooden pins over damp laundry and pondered the past hour or so.

I shuddered at the recollection of the ordeal with Ike McAnn and his horse. No one would hear of the incident from me, and I prayed Ike would be gentleman enough to hold his tongue. But would he? What could be more hilarious than regaling the crowd at the Watering Hole Saloon with a tale of the proper Miss Bishop kicking and screaming in a basket?

Shaking out a pillowslip, my eye caught sight of Wally slinking behind the trees at the far edge of the hotel yard. This introduced another thought. How could I handle a boy like Wally? A teacher must have a well-planned program to hold the attention of her pupils, I knew. Were there any books in Prospect?

My apprehension over being the first teacher in Prospect diverted my thoughts from Ike. He didn't cross my mind again until I saw him catch Rose Hawkins in a swoon nearly on our doorstep.

Rose proved to be the name of the madonna-like lady I had seen at the Sunday services. In fact, I discovered that she was Mrs. Skillings' younger sister.

Evidently Gertie's anxiety over Wally's education had pushed her to immediate action. For while Emmylou and I were reviving ourselves with a cup of tea that afternoon, Mrs. Skillings thrust her black-bonneted head through the doorway and sang out, "Hello, the house."

On our invitation she marched in, shadowed by her sister, Rose, whom she immediately introduced. Rising, we offered our callers our chairs.

While sliding mine toward Rose, I glanced into her eyes. They were blue, slightly protruding and as cold as marbles. She seated herself rigidly and returned my smile with a look of pure hatred. Repelled, I retreated to the bed and balanced on its edge.

Mrs. Skillings' commanding tones caught my attention. "Now, Miss Bishop, I trust you are aware of your God-given responsibility as a teacher of young minds. I fully agree with Mrs. McGinnis that our children need a school. And it appears you are the most qualified person in this isolated location but," she paused, leaned forward, and stabbed a black-gloved finger at me, "your conduct must be above reproach."

"Yes, Mrs. Skillings," I agreed.

She folded her hands in her lap and continued, "I know Reverend Golden well, and he is like his Lord. He uses his hands in carpentry. It seems he has agreed to put together some benches and tables for your pupils. He will also take charge of their spiritual training. School will begin a week from today. Of course, I will need to review all your lesson plans before that time."

Thinking I'd rather withstand a steam engine, I repeated, "Yes, Mrs. Skillings."

Emmylou moved into the circle of women bearing two steaming cups of tea. Her kind, ruddy face, ringed with tangled wisps of hair, looked angelic to me.

It appeared Mrs. Skillings thought otherwise. She drew herself up and said accusingly, "I don't believe we've met formally. You weren't in church yesterday, were you? You do know the Bible commands us to gather together, don't you?"

"No, I warn't there. Would ya take a little sweetnin' in your tea?" Emmylou asked with a twinkle in her eyes. "Might do ya some good."

Emmylou filled in the heavy silence that followed that remark with cheerful accounts of the laundry business.

Our callers rapidly disposed of their tea and rose to leave. I almost resigned my new position when Mrs. Skillings told me in parting, "Mrs. McGinnis thinks there might be fifteen children coming to school so I told Rose she should assist you. Of course, a competent teacher could manage that small number, but Rose needs to occupy her time. Idle hands are the devil's workshop, you know."

Mrs. Skillings bobbed her head to Rose, thus directing my attention that way also. Two red spots stood out on the mother-of-pearl cheeks and a blue vein throbbed beside her right eyebrow. Otherwise she still appeared as carved marble.

Rose followed her sister out the door. Mrs. Skillings had already made her way to the boardwalk in front of our cabin when Rose peered down the walk in the opposite direction, suddenly groaned and pitched herself into Ike McAnn's arms.

"That weren't no faint," Emmylou concluded as she and I discussed it later. "She jest wanted to be hugged up by a handsome man."

Rose had hung limp as a rag doll once Ike's arms had enfolded her. Emmylou had dashed for her smelling salts while I had stared at the scene in front of me, unsure of its implications. Ike had grinned like the cat that caught the canary—and by the gleam in his eye he liked the looks of the bird he'd ensnared. With her hateful eyes closed and her hard features softened, she *was* lovely.

The romantic picture had dissolved into an ugly scene as soon as Mrs. Skillings missed Rose's presence at her heels. She swung about, stomped over to Rose's limp form and smartly slapped her cheek. Rose's eyes flew open as she struggled to regain her footing.

Mrs. Skillings had glared at Ike and ordered, "You unhand her, you masher! Don't you know the Bible says it's not good for a man to touch a woman?"

With that she grabbed Rose by the arm and propelled her down the sidewalk without a backward glance.

Ike shook his head, looking like a man caught in a dream not of his own making and ambled off in the other direction.

"Well, I'll be blamed," Emmylou exclaimed.

Chapter 7

The groaning of the ironing board and the aroma of slightly scorched cotton provided the background for my lesson planning. Hunched over my lap writing desk, brow furrowed, I penned my thoughts. Numbers must be mastered before addition, subtraction and so forth, just as a student needed to know the alphabet before tackling reading. And geography, wasn't that important? I could see some immediate basic needs such as reading, arithmetic and spelling books, a blackboard, maps, slates or paper, and pencils.

Straightening into a stretch, I tapped the end of my nose with my pen and watched Emmylou drop a cool bottom from her ironing handle back onto the hot stove top. The stove lid jumped under its weight while she efficiently clamped her handle on another black base, this one sizzling hot.

Beads of perspiration dotted her flushed face. "Are ya gettin' it all wrote down?" she asked.

"Oh, I'm not sure," I fretted.

"Jest do the best ya can," she advised.

"Gertie sent over a few books left from her attempts to teach Wally and Ben. I gather Ben absorbed something but Wally wasn't very cooperative. I've just finished writing a letter to Aunt Dolly. I thought she might ask around Oak Grove and find some school texts that aren't being used. I know we had some old books of Joe's and mine stored in the attic. I'm sure Flora won't want them."

"Did ya tell your Aunt Dolly that you're the new schoolmarm?"

"Oh yes. I'm sure knowing that will go a long way toward putting her mind at rest. I just added that marriage didn't seem expedient at this time."

Emmylou cocked her head to one side as I rubbed my stiff neck and continued, "I'm going to put this up and lay those dress goods out. I'm sure it won't be the most stylish, but if I keep with it we can have a new dress for you to wear to church Sunday."

"Ya know," Emmylou reflected, "I can't call to mind ever owning a dress that weren't cut from something else or wore by somebody else. This one," she grinned and curtsied, lifting its faded skirt, "was give to me by the sheriff's wife."

"Really?" I asked in astonishment.

Lifting the folded yards of cotton from one of my trunks, I wished it were silk. But I comforted myself with the thought that it was good quality percale. And the print, rose flowers strewn among dainty green leaves, was charming. I'd dip into my funds and see what could be purchased at the Prospect Emporium. Ribbons, lace and buttons for the dress, and perhaps white lawn for petticoats and a chemise.

Humming, I draped the goods across our table.

Arranging the pattern pieces I'd altered the evening before, I took bold whacks with my shears. I barely missed cutting off the end of my thumb when Emmylou shrieked and heaved the iron across the room against the woodbox.

Dumbfounded, I feared for a moment that she'd taken leave of her senses.

"That there rat! I'd like to skin him alive. Did ya know he ate almost a whole bag of my slippery elm bark? And I doubt I'll be able to lay hands on more way out here in the Rocky Mountains."

Quickly recovering her usual good humor, she added, "Maybe he was took with stomach complaint."

Joining her at our stack of firewood, I peered into the shadowy recesses and asked, "Did you hit him? And are you sure it was a rat that ate your cures?"

"You bet your life it was a rat! He left his droppings and if I ain't missin' my guess, it smelt like a pack rat. And course I didn't git him. A rat ain't nobody's fool."

During the noon meal, while chomping herself through enough food for a harvest hand, Gertie shared a list of potential students she had compiled. It included the name of every family in Prospect with children of school age.

"There are a handful of families living up creeks and canyons whose menfolk are engaged in mining and logging, but we'd best forget them," she advised. "The trails would be impassable for youngsters as soon as the fall rains and winter snowstorms set in."

She'd listed seven families on a sheet of paper. Under each family name she'd written the name and age of their school children.

"Do tell, I talked to every one of them and they'll pay two bits a week for every young'un. Now," she continued around a mouthful of potato, "you ain't a-gonna get rich but with me givin' you grub and living quarters, you oughta make it through the winter."

Pausing in her chewing, she gave me a hard stare and confessed, "I'm still as curious as a cat about what brought a refined young lady like you to a place like Prospect. But... if you can give our young'uns some schooling, I'm just thankin' my lucky stars."

I squirmed as guilt enveloped me. Before it completely strangled me, Gertie patted my hand. "Now don't let that upset you none. The lion's share of folks hereabout got something smelly buried in their past."

I looked into sympathetic eyes, recessed into a dumpling face and nearly unloaded all the details concerning my arrival in Prospect. Then I caught myself. How could I explain my association with a murderess? Perhaps Gertie would hold with that maxim, 'Birds of a feather flock together.'

Averting my eyes I studied the paper containing the names and ages of my future pupils.

McGinnis	*Crawford*
Walter - 12	Daniel - 7
Benjamin - 10	
Sally - 6	*Fletcher*
	Carolyn - 8
Golden	Charles - 7
Rebecca - 6	Elizabeth - 6

Bristow	Skillings
Alice - 12	Mary - 10
Orville - 11	Martha - 10
James - 9	Ruth - 8
Florence - 6	

Furners

??

Loftus

Pearl - 8

Puzzling over the last family listed, I asked, "Don't you know the names of the children in the Furners family?"

"No, I don't. They live clean down by the river and my feet were screaming at me by the time I left the Fletchers'. Can't understand their jabberin' nohow. Inviting them into the school is chancy with their furren ways."

"Are you saying this is a family of foreigners, someone from a foreign country?"

In the act of washing down a mouthful of food, Gertie nearly choked on her coffee. "Naturally they's from a furren country, that's how come they's furners."

I couldn't keep from smiling.

Gertie's next observation took me by surprise. "Mercy, you oughta smile more. Remember, honey catches more flies than vinegar."

Her remark caused my smile to progress to a chuckle, then to an unrestrained laugh. Refreshed, I said, "If we're going to hold school, let's include everyone. Exactly how do I find their home?"

Gertie fell in with my plans. "You take Peggy with you. She's been there before. They ain't Irish but they both have the same religion. The one where the Pope's the big chief. You come by and get Peggy along about two. She'll have the kitchen readied by then and I won't need her to be startin' supper for a couple hours."

Peggy, stiff as a newly starched dress, waited for me on the hotel's porch. Greeting me with a formal curtsy, she said, " 'Tis God's blessing upon you I be askin', Miss Bishop."

With her eyes downcast she took the lead. We crossed the road and found a narrow path angling between the bushes and trees. I searched my mind for conversational material but her attitude discouraged intimacy.

Finally I asked, "Do you speak these people's language?"

Without missing a step, she answered, "Faith and 'tis not me that be understanding their tongue. 'Tis love that speaks, you'll be havin' to remember."

How sweet, I thought, as the path deteriorated to a rutted ditch meandering around boulders and outcroppings topped with low-growing shrubs. The bushes, decked in autumn oranges and golds, contrasted pleasantly with the excessive green in this land of evergreens.

As the path progressed toward the river and dropped to an almost perpendicular angle, I discovered these sturdy bushes kept me from slipping to the bottom of the path on my backside. I'd grab a slender branch, often stripping the leaves off, and dig my heels into the earth as I inched my way to the next bush.

Being as agile as a mountain goat, Peggy skimmed down the path until she'd put several yards between us. Turning about, she watched my cautious descent with wide-eyed concern. Retracing her steps, she offered her hand.

As Emmylou had once said, Peggy looked like a pound of soap after a hard week's washing, and even I at one hundred pounds, felt big and ungainly beside her diminutive figure. Her slight arm supported me well, however, and I reached the foot of the hill without mishap.

My need of help went a long way toward removing the wall between us and I was Miss Mercy instead of Miss Bishop by the time she called my attention to the house squatting on the riverbank. Its swaying, mossy roof testified of an ancient age. Some itinerant trapper or miner must have thrown it together while the railroad and Prospect were still someone's dream, I decided.

It appeared deserted. But Peggy marched through the waist high weeds to the door and stuck her head in its opening. "Hellooo, 'tis me-self, Peggy O'Brien, that 'tis here."

Creeping along behind, I followed her through the doorway into the cavelike interior. As my eyes adjusted, I became aware of details. The only sources of light were the open door and a feeble fire in the fireplace at one end of the room. A pot hanging over the smoky flames belched forth a spicy, eye-watering aroma. Then I noticed several children shrinking into the corners like mice.

Peggy walked to a corner where an inert figure lay obscured by a heap of bedding. She launched into a frenzy of unintelligible mutterings and murmurings before wheeling about and propelling me through the door.

Once outside again, she fluttered through a sign of the cross, flung a prayer skyward, and exclaimed, " 'Tis past believin', but 'tis a doctor that poor woman be needin' and I'm afearing the last rites. And not a Father betwixt and between. Sure and I wouldn't be knowin', but my own dear mother looked the same on her death bed, God rest her soul. It's me that be askin', would Miss Brown be willing to care for her?"

Her words so startled me that for a moment I couldn't recall who Miss Brown might be. Collecting myself, I said, "Oh Peggy, I know Emmylou would be happy to come. You run ahead and get her. I'd only hamper you."

While I waited for their return, I felt as useless as one of the fir trees. What could I do? A silence so loud it rang in my ears gave the impression of aloneness. Yet within a few feet cowered several other humans, one of them suffering. Language is a formidable barrier, I thought. But God understands the suffering heart, I reminded myself, and petitioned Him to comfort those within the cabin.

Flopping on a log, I strained my ears to listen, but fortunately the invalid didn't cry out. Perhaps she was beyond that, I worried. I became aware of a slight stirring of needle-laden boughs and gurgling water before my attention was drawn to the path. Peggy sprang into view, as graceful as a deer, with Emmylou hard on her heels.

Emmylou's chin had a determined set to it, and she bounded through the door without pausing to so much as catch her breath. She carried her battered black leather bag in one hand.

Peggy slipped out moments later and suggested we go back to town. "Faith and 'tis me that's believin' Miss Brown needs no help. She be flappin' her hands so's to show the older child what to do. 'Tis the older boy and the man of the house that be out in the woods cutting railroad ties." Peggy explained. "And 'tis me that's needed back to the hotel to get supper."

Emmylou did not return for supper. Gertie, who said she liked to know "what was what," sent Ben down to the house near the river for information.

Later, reliable Ben puffed into the hotel kitchen to tell Gertie, Peggy, and me that, "Miss Brown says there ain't a blamed thing anybody can do, except those on speaking terms with God can pray."

I caught myself smiling at Ben's excellent impersonation of Emmylou's speech.

Dashing the hair from his eyes, he continued, "She says not to look for her until we see her, and if she needs anything she'll send one of the young'uns up. If we see one of them, we're to come even if the young'un doesn't open his mouth. She's kinda up a stump with all that furren jabbering, but she just shows them what she wants by jumping around," he finished.

I lit the lamp as soon as I arrived home. It was still early evening but the shorter days made the interior dim, and I hoped the friendly glow would discourage rats and the other vile guests my mind's eye could visualize.

Seating myself at the table, I threaded a needle and began stitching the gores of Emmylou's dress. I'd finished one seam and begun another when a rap on the door startled me. Cautiously rising and tiptoeing toward the door, I scolded myself. Why be alarmed by a caller? After all, it wasn't even dark yet and this was the middle of a civilized town.

Nevertheless, I tugged on the door with some reluctance. The stubborn door occupied so much of my attention that I didn't glance at my visitor until it stood halfway open. Looking up, I saw a good-sized wooden box tucked under a long arm. As my eyes continued to travel upward—way up—I came to Levi Miller's narrow face. Our eyes met. His were blue, deep blue, and appeared apprehensive. He looked as frightened as a five-year-old on the school steps opening day.

For a long minute neither of us spoke, then my manners overrode my reticence. "Won't you come in, Mr. Miller?"

As he placed one foot over the threshold, his words tumbled over one another. "Miss Brown told me Sunday that you were being bothered by rats. I brought a trap."

Stepping aside, I said, "Bring it in. I do hope it works. Just this morning we saw one behind the woodbox. Emmylou believes it took some of her medicinal herbs."

His brown hair brushed the ceiling poles as he came in. Looking at his long, slender feet, he asked, "Where do you want it set?"

"Maybe you'd better decide and then tell me how to operate the trap," I suggested. "As you can see, we are quite crowded. And on wash days Emmylou's tubs and the dirty laundry take up most of the space."

Still clutching the box, he peered around and decided, "That corner by the woodbox looks good."

I followed him to the corner where he squatted, while I leaned over the woodpile and observed.

He fished out some sticks fitted together in the shape of a four. Holding them up, he said, "This is why the trap is called a figure four trap." Demonstrating, he said, "You prop the box open by resting the edge of the box on the point of the four, then you stick some bait on the prong, like this. Then when the rat smells the salt pork, or whatever, he grabs it and the motion causes the figure to collapse, and you've caught Mr. Rat inside the box."

While engrossed in his instructions, he'd sounded relaxed and comfortable, but as soon as he lifted his eyes to look at me stretched over the loosely stacked wood, he fidgeted and stammered. " 'Course . . . 'course the unhandy part is getting rid of the rat. He's still kicking inside that box and a rat can chew through wood mighty fast."

I found myself stammering also. "How . . . how do you kill it then?"

He shifted his long legs. "Well, I generally use a revolver. Do you have one?"

"A gun?" I asked in wide-eyed horror.

A corner of his mouth quivered and I detected a twinkle in his eyes. *Does he find me amusing?* I wondered, just as the round stick I was resting on gave way.

My feet flew up and I began to roll across the stack of wood. Immediately, Levi's lanky limbs flew into action and his strong fingers spanned my waist, lifting me to my feet. Before I completely regained my equilibrium, the hands jerked back as though burned.

"Oh, how humiliating! And here I was so critical of Rose Hawkins. It seems I've spent more time down than up this past week. Oh . . . oh," I wailed as I burst into tears.

In the midst of my emotional upheaval, Mr. Miller consoled me. "Don't take on so. In God's providence, we all have our ups and downs."

Somewhat mollified, I gulped, "Please forgive me. Only my pride has been injured. And the Proverbs do say, 'Pride goeth before a fall.' Someday I'll learn not to think of myself more highly than I ought, I hope."

While I scrubbed at my face with a handkerchief, Mr. Miller shuffled his feet, cleared his throat and pulled on an ear lobe. "I'd best be going or I'll not make it home before midnight."

I tipped my head back and looked up into his face. "You mean you rode all the way from your ranch to bring that trap?"

"I had other business, too. By the way, where is Miss Brown? She seems to have cured Sally's cat."

"Emmylou is down by the river doctoring a poor woman who is very ill. Peggy and I discovered her when we went to call. We felt there might be some children in the family for the school."

"Gertie told me about your school. Could you use some more books? I have several."

Tired of craning my neck, I suggested, "Let's be seated and have a cup of tea. I'd like to talk to you about the school."

Evidently the idea of drinking tea with a lady was too intimate, for he stammered his farewells and strode to the door, only to be trapped by its refusal to budge.

Instead of falling apart as I feared, he accepted the challenge and yanked the door open so he could reach the top. Borrowing our hatchet, he used his excessive height to advantage. Standing flat-footed, he shaved off the top edge of the plank that was catching on the door sill.

As he returned the hatchet to me, I laid my hand

over his bony fingers and murmured, "Thank you, Mr. Miller. You have been so kind."

A flush spread across his face to the roots of his hair and continued to the tips of his ears. Nodding briefly, he leapt down the steps and disappeared into the night.

Lost in thought, I closed the door with ease. What a strange man. Prospect, Montana positively oozed with peculiar people. Peculiar, yes, but most were nice. I was confident that Levi Miller wouldn't publish my humiliation.

Before crawling into bed, I studied the trap and decided not to set it until Emmylou came home. What if I caught a rat the first thing?

Her arrival pulled me out of a deep sleep. Noisy muttering and shoe slinging cleared all fuzziness from my brain, replacing it with concern.

"That mean-spirited old cow!" she fumed.

Fully awake, I asked, "Are you talking about the foreign lady?"

"No!" Emmylou snarled. I heard a seam rip as she jerked her dress over her head. "I'm talkin' about that hoity-toity mayor's wife. The furren man showed up to home. There ain't nothin' anybody kin do fer that woman. She's a-dyin'. And her man asked me to see if the preacher'd leg it down fer something called last rites since there ain't a blackrobe in the county."

"So," Emmylou continued in a tight voice, "I goes to his door and asks for the parson and that old busybody Mrs. Skillings and a couple other ladies is having tea. She noses right in afore he could even open his mouth. Said that were a heathen practice and the Reverend don't dabble in witchcraft. Then she jest elbows him outa the way and starts spewin'

111

out Bible talk 'til I took off before I plastered her one in the mug."

Still trembling at the encounter, Emmylou dropped to the side of the bed.

"It's a good thing that parson ran after me and said he'd be happy to go to their place, or you'd a-never catched me in your church come Sunday!"

A wave of sympathy swept over me. Under its influence, I padded over to the stove, fanned the embers into life and heated water for tea.

While the tea worked its cure on Emmylou, I shared most of Levi Miller's visit with her. By the time I came to the part where he fixed the door, I noticed, to my relief, that a bit of her old sparkle had returned.

Sitting there on the edge of the bed, tea cup resting on her knee, she said mysteriously, "Fer cryin' out loud, Mercy. Don't give that there red checkered tablecloth away. Ya may be needin' it yet."

I pondered her comment a long time. She didn't seem to be seeking revenge on Levi after all.

Chapter 8

"Don't let that old she-goat push ya in no corner," Emmylou admonished while waving me out the door Saturday morning. Time had run out. With school scheduled to open Monday, I couldn't postpone my conference with Mrs. Skillings any longer.

Briskly, I walked down the street to the Skillings' home, a white frame house, and made my way up the steps to the porch. My tap on the door was answered by identical twin girls.

Solemnly they stood, swathed in grease-spattered aprons that brushed their shoe tops. Perhaps they'd be able to lay some claim to beauty after they'd grown into their overlarge noses and long front teeth, I thought. Or learned to smile.

Recalling Gertie's advice, I smiled and graciously accepted the invitation to enter.

Stepping inside, my eyes widened, then blinked not once, but twice. What a shambles! I paused, carefully selecting a pathway between obstacles. A bucket on the floor was partially filled with murky water. On the bucket's rim a string mop rested, its handle jutting out to trip the unwary.

Another girl, younger than the twins, ushered me to a kitchen chair. While I wavered between whether to remove a corset from the chair or ignore its presence, the girl swept it to the floor. Her infectious grin and chirpy little voice almost made me anxious for Monday morning.

"Hi, I'm Ruthie," her round face became even rounder as her grin widened.

"Miss Bishop, scoot your chair around here," a voice dictated. I recognized it as belonging to Mrs. Skillings, but it took me a moment to locate her. She was seated on the opposite side of the table, hidden from view by mountains of objects. In a swift survey, I identified a galvanized washing tub, a lantern, a butter churn and an assortment of food-encrusted dishes. A collapsed umbrella balanced atop the churn.

After finding her, I decided she blended in well with her surroundings. Instead of the well-groomed matron she presented outside these walls, her uncorseted flesh was shrouded in a stained brown housewrapper. And surely her hair hadn't seen the business side of a comb this morning, I thought, as I waited for her to finish writing on a paper which was resting on a small patch of table surface.

She flung her pen aside and with eyes blazing through her spectacles, she shouted, "Hallelujah! Now that we have a real church in this town, I've been thinking about what the women of Prospect could do to further the kingdom. And I've found the answer."

She halted abruptly to throw an order over her shoulder, "Mary, Martha, watch that meat. It's burning."

As she spoke, I saw a blue haze hovering over the stove as an accompanying charred odor reached my nostrils.

Ignoring her domestic problems, Mrs. Skillings pursued her earlier conversation. "As an instructor of young minds, I realized you'd want to be first to sign the pledge." And shoving her paper under my nose, she handed me her pen.

Bewildered, I answered, "Mrs. Skillings, I'm afraid I don't understand. What pledge?"

"Why, the pledge of the Women's Christian Temperance Union, naturally. But, foolish me, you've no doubt signed it in your home town in Iowa."

"No, I've never signed it. I felt it unnecessary. I've never been troubled by strong drink," I told her defensively.

Dragging her chair closer, she thrust her beaklike nose at me and lectured. "Not necessary for you perhaps, but sorely needed for those gripped by its power. Are you aware, young lady, that there are three saloons in Prospect? And this only a small town of two hundred souls. The evil influences those saloons have on the men, women and children are beyond imagining. I considered organizing a Ladies Aid but discounted that as being mere busy work. Those lost souls don't need quilts and platters of cookies. They need victory from the demon of alcohol!"

Shrinking back into my chair, I meekly wrote my name below the national pledge: "I hereby solemnly promise, God helping me, to abstain from all distilled, fermented and malt liquors, including wine, beer and cider, and to employ all proper means to discourage the use and traffic of the same."

As soon as I'd written the "p" in Bishop, I regretted the act. What would Mrs. Skillings consider *proper means*? My stomach fluttered and I despised myself for once again letting others dictate my actions.

Satisfied, Mrs. Skillings crossed her arms and relaxed. An elfin on tiptoes danced up to her but instead of hugging that scrap of humanity, she leaped into action. Snatching up a fly swatter, she banished the little girl as would a lion tamer at a circus. "Mary, Martha, Ruth, Leah, are you performing your duties?" she shouted. "Where's your baby brother?"

She hopped up and looked through narrowed eyes, searching the room. Obviously, this was an old game to the children. Bodies darted from one spot to another as in a game of Hide and Seek, when "it" yells "ready or not here I come." Even the elfin slipped under the table.

Embarrassed, I looked away and spied Rose, looking like a tidy doll in the midst of this chaos, plying her needle. I found myself more sympathetic toward her. Perhaps her aloof manner was the only armor the poor girl possessed.

Panting, Mrs. Skillings dropped her fly swatter and settled back into her chair. I pulled myself together and produced my lesson plans.

She dismissed them with a wave. "With your background, I'm sure you'll do an adequate job with the a-b-c's and so forth. I'm more concerned that you instill a moral bent in those young minds. I

116

know you're pious but I'm not easy in my mind about that woman you reside with. One can't be too careful of their companions. Perhaps you don't know that she leans toward strange beliefs."

I sputtered to life. "But Mrs. Skillings! She was merely helping a lady on her deathbed."

"Now, now, don't get riled. I'm sure Miss Brown asked for those pagan rites while under emotional stress. But her language—vile!"

"Emmylou isn't responsible for her upbringing," I defended, grateful that this woman didn't know of her notorious past.

"No, but she's an adult now and answerable for her actions. I'm only cautioning you as a mother would," she soothed.

Not trusting myself to respond, I excused myself.

Seeing me to the door, she promised, "I'll keep you informed as to the plans and activities of our Temperance Union. I plan to recruit as many women as possible and we'll not rest until the doors are locked on every saloon and the men return to the bosoms of their families."

What of the many men in Prospect who have no families? I pondered, as I picked my way down the steps. I wanted no part in her Temperance Union. So why hadn't I stood on my own two feet instead of being bullied into joining? Hadn't Aunt Dolly said temperance unions got the cart before the horse? I wished I'd had more backbone.

Could Mrs. Skillings have prophetic powers? I asked myself that very evening when Emmylou announced that she, Ike and George were going to "do the town." I wasn't in the dark long as to what that involved.

The two men arrived on the heels of Emmylou's announcement. Ike breezed in, snapping his fingers. He looked more handsome than ever, with his dark hair falling into shiny waves and his leaf green vest setting off broad shoulders and a trim waist. Hoss trailed behind, looking as though he was on his way to a funeral.

Ike tried to include me in their plans. With an exaggerated bow, he said, "Mercy, why don't you honor our company with your presence? If you don't care to indulge in spirits, you can play the piano for us. Far as I know, the only piano in Prospect resides in the National Saloon. And I hear you tickle the ivories real sweet. Otherwise, we have to listen to Big Mick. And his sausage fingers on those keys assault a person's eardrums."

Shocked, I asked, "Are you suggesting that a lady go into a saloon?"

Soft as a caress, he laid his hand on my clenched fist. The scent of bay rum shaving soap took me back to the Bishop Place and Father dressed for a lodge meeting.

"Don't look so offended. It won't kill you. Might do you some good. Loosen you up a bit."

Falling back on "How to Discourage A Skirt Chaser—Lesson #5," Miss Prince's Female Academy, I struck a pose worthy of an A+.

Disheartened, he turned away and changed the subject.

"Caught any rats in that box yet? That Levi comes up with the wildest ideas. Say, do you know what the 500 pound mouse said?"

When no one responded, he told us anyway. "Here kitty, kitty."

"Oh, fer crying out loud, come on, Ike," Emmylou

said in exasperation. "The night's not gittin' any younger."

Tucking one hand into Ike's arm, she fluttered her other hand in my direction, then tugged at Hoss's sleeve.

Left alone with my thoughts and time to finish Emmylou's dress, I brooded. Emmylou's loose morals upset me but what she needed was a changed heart, and only God could do that. Then she would be a new creature. And what better place to hear of her need than in church? I reasoned.

Taking heart, I not only finished Emmylou's dress, but pressed and arranged it on a hanger looped over a nail on the wall.

I went to bed, satisfied I'd done my part in assuring Emmylou's presence in church the next morning.

Never pin your hopes on a dress, I fumed, ramming my hat on my head, preparatory to leaving for church.

Always before Emmylou had been an early riser, but when the clock had read nine and she hadn't twitched, I had tapped her on the shoulder. She'd mumbled, stirred and then nestled further into the bedcovers.

Impatiently I'd flipped the covers back and spoken into her exposed ear. "Emmylou, it's time to get up and get ready for church. Your dress is all ready for you."

One bloodshot eye studied me. A sour stench, not unlike some old beer barrels Father had stored at the Bishop Lumberyard, prickled my nose. She said thickly, "I'm stayin' in this here bed. My head feels like its gonna bust open."

Perhaps it's for the best, I decided. How would

Mrs. Skillings react if Emmylou attended church in that pickled condition? So what if no one appreciated my sacrifices? Why feel persecuted over needle-pricked fingers and a shrunken purse? Nonetheless, I left for church feeling like a suffering saint.

In the store building, warm voices and open hands reached out to me. Putting a few more names to faces restored much of my sense of well-being.

Levi directed us in songs I'd sung since I was chin-high to a church pew and nostalgia played with my heart strings. Still running on my emotions, I longed for heaven after Parson Golden graphically pictured the new heaven and new earth spoken of in Revelation.

Those lofty sentiments took flight, however, when Mrs. Skillings appropriated the pulpit and shook her temperance cause under our noses. Before surrendering the pulpit to Reverend Golden for his closing remarks, she shared "an uplifting" little poem.

> I stand for prohibition
> The utter demolition
> Of all this curse of misery and woe
> Complete extermination
> Entire annihilation
> The saloon must go!

I wrinkled my nose in distaste just as Ike, two rows ahead and looking better than Emmylou had, laughingly whispered in Rose's ear. A tight squeezing of the heart didn't denote jealousy did it? Or did I entertain aspirations of reforming him? Come now, Mercy! I chided myself.

I learned upon my arrival home that Emmylou had been summoned to the foreigner's home, the Paskas'. There she had watched "that poor woman depart this here world, and her so far from home."

Our differences forgotten, I wept with Emmylou.

The first day of school arrived with the next morning. But low gray clouds threatening rain hid the mountains as I stepped forth, fortified with a liberal splash of lilac blossom perfume.

Letting myself into the store/church building an hour before school was to begin, I squared my shoulders and marched up to my desk which had been yesterday's pulpit. I looked about. Due to darkness brought on by the gathering storm, the empty corners of the room were vague, shadowy blotches. The faint light coming through the long store windows appropriately highlighted the crude benches and tables under the sills. This would be the scene of action, and I prayed the drama would not prove a tragedy.

Removing my jacket, I draped it over one of the nails furnished in lieu of coat hooks. The cheerful snapping and popping of the pot-bellied stove lifted my spirits and I silently thanked the Reverend Golden.

Returning to my desk, I seated myself and pored over "Lesson Plans For Day One." After several minutes, my eyes strayed to the books stacked on the corner of the table. Levi had loaded them into my arms after church the day before. He'd only had time to run his long fingers through his carefully combed hair when Mrs. Skillings had hustled him off without even an apology.

I doubted my pupils would be ready for *The Complete Works of Shakespeare*, but the ragged little volume, *National Pictorial Primer For Children*, would be invaluable.

Glancing at my Plans once more, I took the chalk provided and turned to the splotch of black painted across the rough wall behind my desk. Easing the chalk over and around knotholes and cracks, I lettered my name and had begun on the date when the door swung open and the Skillings' children bounded through.

My heart sank, I'd counted on this extra time.

The younger family members scattered like buckshot while Mary and Martha, heavy with responsibility, stalked up to me.

Without preamble, one twin said, "Ma sent the two young'uns with us 'cause she went with Pa out to Mr. Miller's."

"They're building fence," the other twin added.

"And Aunt Rose says she's sick and can't come to help you," twin number one said.

"But she's gotta get out of bed to cook supper," said twin number two with satisfaction.

Twin number one continued with a smirk. "We saw her and Mr. McAnn out behind the McGinnis barn while Ma was out calling for the Temperance Union last night."

With their feet planted squarely on the floor, the twins presented a united front as they declared in unison, "We told Aunt Rose we'd tell Ma about her and Mr. McAnn if she don't get supper."

"Oh my," I sighed, lost for words. What did one say to ten-year-olds with such spiteful faces?

The question was answered for me when their baby brother grabbed the water bucket. Someone had set it on a chair for the students' drinking water. Flying across the room I managed to catch it in midair and splatter myself in the act.

Shaking droplets from my skirt, I whirled about exasperated. "I cannot conduct a classroom and care for infants at the same time. Mary or Martha, take these two preschoolers back home and tell your aunt I said for her to look after them."

Fifteen minutes after the opening bell I'd abandoned The Plan. I'd written: "Open school with four stanzas of 'We're Marching to Zion.'" Hence, I'd organized sixteen pliable children into orderly lines and, using a Jew's harp, had started them on the right note.

Before we began, I'd suggested they march in place. Only the McGinnis children, the Golden child, and Pearl Loftus sang. The others watched me with awestruck eyes and motionless feet until, with an impish grin, Wally bellowed out, "We're marching!" and stomped his heels into the floor until the windowpanes clattered. Abruptly all heads swiveled as my students beheld this marvel of disrespect.

Naturally, Opening Hymn ground to a halt, but not before Wally had established his position in the classroom.

Out of fairness, I must confess he contained himself most of the day. But all through roll call and the first day task of probing tender minds to discover the extent of previous instruction, he knew, I knew, and each little body enrolled in Prospect School knew—Wally held the whip.

Chapter 9

I was caught. Willingly or not, I found myself wrapped up in my classroom. While many of my neighbors were idled by the October rains, I struggled to keep from drowning in a sea of inexperience. Each morning as I faced sixteen pairs of eyes, I threw a petition heavenward and took roll call.

My students did not remain spellbound little cherubs. Before a week had passed, one child after another shot out of their trance and scattered their sentiments upon the rest of us. Often this proved disruptive. My first days, I spent more time preaching the rules of kindness than the three R's.

No, Wally shouldn't spit tobacco juice on Pearl Loftus' silk sash. But on the other hand, Pearl, the pampered darling of older parents, was not endearing herself to Prospect's "lard and biscuit" children.

In the Bristow family of four, Alice, at twelve, carried a king-sized chip on her bony shoulder and not much of anything in her head. To every question I received a surly, "dunno." Her brother, Orville, "who thunked he were eleven," spent his school days paying homage to Wally, while poor James, with his vacant, crossed eyes, lived somewhere beyond touch. Their little sister, Flossy, was registered in my primary class. In spite of the nasty cough that racked her thread-like body, I held to the dream that I could inspire her mind.

Also in my primary class was little Sally McGinnis, Ruthie from the Skillings family, and shy little Becky Golden, the preacher's oldest child. Ruthie, with her cheery grin, minus both front teeth, and Becky, the frail thumbsucker, begged for hugs and found me with a steady supply.

Tiny Danny Crawford sported a sweptback cowlick, teasing eyes and an uncanny ability to prick the tender spots of the ill-humored. The three Fletcher children, Betty, Charles, and John, completed my beginning class. They were shy and smelled of soap and loving care. This, my largest group, tugged at my heart strings until I nearly toppled over in my desire to see them progress.

Yet, even they, like kittens in a box, could bare their claws and spit.

My three ten-year-olds completed the enrollment. Serious natured Ben McGinnis absorbed knowledge like a sponge. And Mary and Martha Skillings didn't tolerate nonsense from anyone, including the teacher.

Nor their aunt. From the information they freely dispensed, I gathered Rose continued to keep company with Ike. And the twins, not to let a good thing slip through their fingers, enjoyed respite from cooking the evening meal.

Reluctantly, Rose put in an appearance at school nearly every day. But she left me with no doubt as to her position. "I can't abide children. They give me nervous prostration." And after she had proved her point by slapping James for walking on her toes, I left her to her own devices. This mainly consisted of sitting in the corner and manicuring her nails, doing needlework, or reading books of which Flora would approve—*On Her Wedding Morn* or *A Mad Love.*

In spite of my misgivings about my qualifications, the "Weekly Prospect" featured me as a model schoolmistress. I prepared to read the account from the newspaper while Emmylou and I relaxed one evening amidst the wet sheets which crisscrossed our cabin.

Immersed as we had been in getting settled and school starting, neither of us had had much time to wonder about the author of our identical letters. Tonight we had mentioned it again and then decided only time would reveal the culprit. Changing the subject, I said, "Oscar Skillings, the editor of the newspaper, interviewed me after school Monday. I think the account is a bit flamboyant."

"I feel right sorry for that man, bein' married and all to that Missus of his," Emmylou said. "He's a right enough gent. Ran into him one day when I were drummin' up some more washin' business.

"Ways I sees it," she changed the subject without realizing it, "with all these here bachelors in town, some of 'em should be willin' to part with a few shekels to get out of scrubbin'."

I wrinkled my nose. "Judging by the odor, I don't believe the majority care much."

I admired Emmylou's ambition, but attempting to carry on a daily routine in a cramped cabin was discouraging enough without the additional hazard of being strangled by the leg of some man's underdrawers. The inclement weather had forced her to do the clothes drying on lines secured over our heads.

Emmylou poked a chapped finger at the newspaper and said, "Well, what do that newsrag have to say?"

I tilted the paper toward the lamp's pool of light and read.

" 'Another first in our flourishing city of Prospect, Montana. On September 29th, a school was organized in the vacant store building owned by Mr. Levi Miller of Bear Canyon. Sixteen children are enrolled under the expert tutelage of Miss Mercy Bishop, late of Oak Grove, Iowa.

" 'This reporter observed the class in session and was greatly impressed with the quality of education our younger citizens are receiving. Miss Bishop is ably assisted by Miss Rose Hawkins.

" 'Our esteemed schoolmistress resides with another enterprising young lady, Miss Emmylou Brown, formerly of North Dakota. Miss Brown is engaged in a laundry business in their home adjacent to the Prospect Hotel and is soliciting the patronage of the community.

" 'Our fair city can only benefit from the presence of these up-and-coming members of the fairer gender.' "

"Well, I'll be a monkey's uncle," Emmylou exclaimed. "That there makes out we're mighty grand. Last time I were wrote up in a newspaper were during the murder trial."

Ignoring her pleasure, I skimmed down the page. "Mr. Skillings also printed the notice of the organizational meeting of the Temperance Society tomorrow night in the hotel lobby. I shudder when I think that I'm required to attend. Mrs. Skillings collared me after school today and left no doubt as to her wishes."

"Does it say anybody can come?" Emmylou inquired.

"Oh yes, she'll want as many as possible."

"Good," Emmylou said.

Perhaps it will do *you* some good, I thought. As the pelting of the rain on the window intensified, I hopped up to inspect the water level in the tin cans placed to catch the drips trickling through gaps in our shake roof. Emmylou's wish for a waterproof roof had proven futile. Instead, Gertie had supplied us with empty cans from the hotel kitchen. Since the locations of the leaks were subject to change, the cans also shifted positions frequently. As well as our bed. Emmylou said we'd shoved the bed across the floor so many times the legs were a couple inches shorter.

The following evening Emmylou and I remained at the hotel after supper. I crept into the hotel lobby and found a seat on an upended packing box. Evidently Gertie didn't own enough chairs to seat the number of ladies interested in temperance activities, I decided, as I adjusted my skirts, observing the assembling of most of the female members of Prospect.

The ladies entered, shedding water-saturated wraps and goodwill. Before long the hotel lobby sounded like feeding time in a hen house. There weren't many social gatherings for the ladies and they meant to make the most of an evening out.

No one was concerned with style. Submitting to the wet weather, hats had been abandoned for more waterproof gear. One jolly lady bounced in under an upended bucket.

I watched Emmylou make herself part of the group, shaking hands and exchanging opinions as she bustled about the room.

Promptly at seven Mrs. Skillings sailed up to the hotel desk and gave the bell a smart rap. The chatter tapered off but didn't cease until she slapped the bell once more and cleared her throat meaningfully.

Rapidly, seats were located and attentive faces turned toward Mrs. Skillings. She stood before us, arrayed in a well-corseted Sunday silk, sternly sizing us up. In honor of the occasion she wore a good-sized hat devoid of all frills except one feather that waved bravely.

Wasting no time on non-essentials, she whipped out a sheet of paper and began outlining the aims of the Temperance Society. By the time she'd blasted every saloon keeper in town, the jolly mood in the room dissipated. I sighed. Why must *causes* be so grim? From my corner only backs were visible, but they seemed to sag before my eyes.

While my mind strayed from Mrs. Skillings and her soapbox oratory, the women twisted in their seats and, to my horror, I noticed their attention focused on me. I looked at the floor and clutched the edge of the box.

Mrs. Skillings' commanding voice jerked my chin from my chest. "Our teacher, Miss Bishop, sitting in

130

the far corner, was the first to sign the pledge and I'm sure every high-minded lady will desire to follow her example. Carrying out our plan to sit in protest at the door of all three saloons each evening will require the cooperation of all Christian women."

Fortunately for my shaky constitution, interest shifted back to Mrs. Skillings, as she continued to develop her scheme of emptying the "dens of iniquity."

"Every evening we'll place two chairs in front of the door of each saloon. Two of our ladies will occupy these seats. Like avenging angels, we will zealously sing hymns of Zion. We will trust that the men preparing to enter these vile establishments will see our ladies beseeching them and turn from the error of their ways . . . . " At this point she shook her fist at the ceiling. " . . . Turn their backs on the path of sin and return to the bosoms of their families!"

Eyebrows were raised and the ladies shifted in their seats once more. Some whispered opinions were exchanged. Even with her eyes fixed on heaven, Mrs. Skillings couldn't ignore the hesitancy of her troops.

"Be bold against evil!" she exhorted.

This comment loosened the tongues of the women, and before she completely lost our attention she raised her voice and shouted over the babble. "Now, I have a list here at the hotel desk telling each lady when her turn will be and what hymns she and her companion will sing. Remember, rain or snow, we'll suffer for The Cause. Be spectacles for good. If you haven't signed the pledge, hurry and do so. Join the ranks!"

My heart sank. I was sure to be on the top of the

list. At that moment, from the haven of my corner, I thought I'd rather occupy a horse stall—with a horse in it—than be pierced by the eyes of strange men.

Seated up front, Emmylou caught my attention. She winked one brown eye just as Gertie rolled heavily to center stage. Her bulk eased Mrs. Skillings to one side and her trumpeting voice caught everyone's interest. Her arms were wrapped about a plump, rainbow-hued quilt.

She asked, "How many of you have dress goods that could be sewed into a patchwork quilt?"

I remembered the scraps Aunt Dolly had tucked into one of my trunks. My hand joined those of my neighbors.

Gertie chuckled. "Do tell, but that's first rate. The reason I'm asking is there's folks around about us who haven't enough covers for their beds this winter. Nothing I like more than quilting. And as the old saying goes, 'Many hands make light work.' So now that winter's clamping down on us, I'm inviting any of you who sees fit to join me here in the hotel lobby every Tuesday and Thursday after supper's done and we'll piece quilts. According to Peggy, that furren family who's dear mother just passed on are needin' covers. Most of you didn't know about that death 'cause they had the burying up to Wallace where they could have a priest do the speakin' over the grave. But those little mites shouldn't have to suffer chilblains when we women can do something for them."

As enthusiasm bubbled, I scooted off my box and inched my way around and between women in cozy little knots. I greeted anyone who noticed me, but my smile was hypocritical and I didn't let anyone deter me from my path to the desk.

Sure enough, "Miss Mercy Bishop" was listed alongside "Mrs. Daniel Fletcher," under *Monday Evening*. For two hours we were to sing, "Stand Up For Jesus," "Throw Out The Lifeline," "Brighten The Corner," and pray whenever the spirit led, while seated in front of the National Saloon.

Turning my back on the warm, friendly lobby, I slipped through a door into the chilly, dimly-lit hall. Alone, I sank onto the bottom step of the stairs.

Cupping my chin in my hands, I mentally searched for a trusted individual I could consult concerning my confused state. Not Emmylou. I desired to know God's will and she scoffed at Him. Could I confide in Gertie, Peggy, or any of the handful of church attenders I'd met? My knowledge of their Biblical views was sketchy. Once, back home, I'd confided in our pastor's wife when, in my adolescent superiority, I'd looked down my freckled nose at Aunt Dolly's common-sense approach to life. But here in Prospect there was no pastor's wife.

More to the point, was my abhorrence of being a spectacle simply pride? Fear of exposure? Uncertainty gripped me. Could God really be lifted up by my presence at the door of a saloon? Would keeping men from a saloon set them on God's paths, or would a cozy quilt be a better inducement to stay home?

The rasp of the outside door handle brought my endless speculations to an abrupt halt. Jerking to my feet, I steadied myself and fled back to the refuge of the lobby.

I hovered on the fringes of the partylike atmosphere until I spied Peggy, dwarfed by the big enameled coffee pot. Seizing the opportunity to be useful, I passed ginger cookies. Instead of shrinking within myself, I freely exchanged greetings behind my plate of cookies and could name several ladies as potential friends by the time the meeting broke up.

*   *   *

The next day was Friday and competition day at school. I'd created a number of games to test my students' skills and devised ways to involve everyone, even the Bristows.

Alice kept score since she was capable of simple mathematics, while Orville recorded it on the blackboard. To my delight, Flossy kept pace in my beginners class and competition was geared to include that group. James, our cheering section, often applauded the wrong person or group, but all the students kindly tolerated him. Even Wally. He'd mastered the art of pricking ego balloons, but when he encountered James, a mother couldn't have been more tender.

On Fridays my students were like colts in spring, kicking their heels and full of good spirit. Shrieking over victories or groaning under defeat, all aspired to wear the coveted First Place Badge. Emmylou and I had fashioned a gleaming dollar-sized affair using tin snips and an old piece of tin. Rivalry between the self-styled Cougars and Wild Cats was fierce. The winning team earned various privileges for the following week.

We discovered after the first Friday competition that Wally was a poor loser. But on contest day he bowed to the rules; the majority saw to that. This forced him to spend more time studying and less in mischief Monday through Thursday.

On that first Friday, Rose had clapped her hands over her ears and, complaining that our unbridled enthusiasm caused her head to pound, escaped, never to appear again on that last day of our school week.

My head rarely ached on Fridays, but by dismissal time I normally displayed about as much zip as a wet mop. Perhaps I'd have ended the day with more drive if I'd contained myself. Instead, I pranced and whooped about in such a manner that I'm sure Miss Prince of the Female Academy would have fainted dead away at the sight of her honor graduate.

On the Friday following the temperance meeting, I'd forgotten myself completely and thrown my arms around little Charles Fletcher before pinning the First Place Badge on the plaid shirt that covered his expanded chest. Then, the twice-defeated Cougar team won when Flossy Bristow correctly spelled h-o-u-s-e, and I leaped about, exposing too much ankle and punishing my weak hip.

So, not surprisingly, I shuffled home. But the sight of Levi Miller tossing firewood from a wagon bed sent my energy skyward.

We were between rain showers and the sun smiled down as he replenished our shrunken wood supply. Just as I arrived at the corner of the wagon, Levi, who was engrossed in his labors, flung a hunk over his shoulder. Squealing, I side-stepped the flying missile.

Levi spun around, stunned. Then before I could bat an eye he'd coordinated his lanky limbs and pivoted off the wagon bed, landing nimbly at my feet. Anxiously he inquired, "Miss Bishop, you aren't hurt?"

As he leaned down, I looked up into troubled blue eyes and reassured him. "No, not at all."

He stepped away, took a deep breath, then whipped off the old felt hat that rested on his ears. "How do you do?" he asked formally.

I smiled and clasped my books beneath the apple green cape Aunt Dolly had knitted to match my eyes. Feeling as giddy as a schoolgirl, I cooed, "Oh, Mr. Miller, you can't begin to imagine how we appreciate the wood! And you even split it to fit our stove. How kind."

Levi edged backwards until he bumped into the wagon bed, then kneading his poor hat brim, he appeared to cast about for a way of escape.

Feeling slightly guilty for his discomfort, I set the giddy schoolgirl aside and assumed the more proper role of schoolmarm.

"Won't you sit down and rest a minute?" I invited primly.

The corners of his mouth twitched. "Ladies first."

Suddenly drained, I plopped onto an upended piece of wood.

Levi strode over and collapsed like a string puppet atop a welter of wood sticks.

Now that we were as cozy as a courting couple in a parlor, speech deserted us.

Levi combed his long fingers through his hair.

Frantically, I snatched at subjects of common interest. Rat traps, church, the Skillings family. Yes. I'd ask Levi's opinion on closing the saloons.

I bent toward him and dropped my burden in his lap. "Mr. Miller, I'm so upset by the idea of sitting in front of a saloon and singing hymns. But Mrs. Skillings believes this will drive men away from the saloon doors and send them back home. Is she right?"

The sun had set behind the mountains, leaving us with a damp chill before Levi answered. He mutilated his hat some more, pulled on an ear and shot a quick glance my way. Then, cocking his head to one side, he looked into my eyes.

"Well, I'd say yes and no. Yes, they'll be ashamed when they see you ladies and they'll no doubt slink off. Most of them, anyway. But no, it isn't going to make a mite of difference when it's all said and done, to my way of thinking. As soon as you ladies stop sitting there they'll come back like a dog to its kill. I suspect Mrs. Skillings doesn't fully understand about saloons. Me, I make a point of never going into one 'cause some evil things do go on in those places, but the biggest number of men don't go there to get drunk."

At this point he paused and studied me until I grew warm enough inside my apple green cape to consider shedding it. Before this became necessary, however, he continued enlightening me on the social habits of western men.

"Out West, men are lonesome. There aren't many families, clubs, lodges, churches, opera houses nor decent women, so they gather in saloons for entertainment when they aren't working themselves into an early grave. They meet in one of those vile-smelling buildings to play cards, visit, and drink liquor. Mostly, that's all. Like anywhere, there are a few rotten apples. Those places do harbor gamblers, drunks, loose women, fighting and such, but mostly they're just a social club."

After this lengthy speech he was suddenly silent, looking at the toe of his boot.

"But Mr. Miller, you haven't answered my question," I cried. "Do you think *I* should participate?"

"What'll happen if you don't?" he asked in return.

"I guess I hadn't thought that far."

I gave my imagination free reign. "First of all, Mrs. Skillings would be very angry with me. She might try to remove me as teacher. She believes that, as the schoolteacher, I'm the prime example to the other ladies."

Once more looking in my eyes, he asked, "Well, what'll happen if you do take your turn sitting in front of a saloon?"

In my distraction, I addressed him by his given name. "Oh, Levi, I'll simply shrivel up and die! All those strange men watching me make such a fool of myself."

Untangling his legs, he stood up and hovered over me. "Come now, Mercy, the Bible says we can do all things through Christ who strengthens us. Talking to young ladies makes me weak-kneed, but you notice I'm not falling on my face this time."

I peered up through my lashes and caught the flash of a boyish grin.

I answered with a smile of my own, but hung determinedly to my point. "Yes, but why make the effort if it won't influence anyone for God?" I argued.

"You might influence at least one man toward Him. And it won't do any harm that I can think of. God says for us to live at peace with all men, as much as we can. No sense disturbing Mrs. Skillings.

If I don't miss my guess, she'll see how useless this plan is before long. Hearts have to be changed first, then habits follow. But in the meantime you will have obeyed God by submitting to her authority. If it proves to make a mockery of God, then you'll need to obey God rather than man. But give it a try."

As I struggled to rise, Levi reached down for my hand. For some reason, having my hand covered by his affected my breathing. "You're an answer to prayer, Levi. I'm so glad God sent you along. I was at my wit's end."

Irrelevantly he said, "Your hands are cold."

"Yes, it's time I went inside," I said with a decided lack of enthusiasm.

Silently we stared into each other's eyes. After a long moment he released my hands and I went into the cabin.

Chapter 10

Before I could cross Monday off the calendar I had to do my part in Mrs. Skillings' scheme to empty the saloons.

During the night a sharp Northern wind had invaded our little valley. The mercury plunged, causing the rain to turn to sleety snow. To our dismay, Emmylou and I discovered a slight dusting of snow on our quilt top when we awakened. This made me even more appreciative of the warm, dry store/school building. Levi had built it weathertight and the Reverend Golden's snapping fire banished any wandering chills.

Perhaps the heat radiating from the stove, along with scratchy longjohns, irritated little bodies. Or maybe the wind provoked naughty deeds. Whatever the reason, the youngsters were full of pent-up energy. Talking out of turn, Wally informed us that the wind whining around the corners sounded like a hungry dog. This produced a spatter of snickers but I failed to find humor in the statement. A hard stare brought the majority of transgressors into line. A threat that we'd not open the large pasteboard box sitting in the middle of the floor until order was restored quelled the others.

Aunt Dolly had written that she'd badgered all her friends and enemies into donating schoolbooks for her dear niece teaching school out in Montana. Wally had carted the box over from the depot on Saturday, and it rested on the floor like a giant Christmas package.

But children can only restrain themselves so long. When Wally skillfully split the pasteboard open with his pocket knife, tranquility vanished and we all pounced on the treasures it held.

"Whoopee, lookit all them books!"

"Git your elbow outa my eye. I want one of them magazines."

"Oh lookee, Miss Bishop, it tells here how to make paper snowflakes to hang in the window. Could we, please?"

"Hey, here's a story about kings a-fightin' with swords and such."

"Stop trompin' on my toes!"

"Miss Bishop, Wally's shoving."

Before I could assert my authority, Mary said highhandedly, "Hey, all you urchins line up here."

"Yeah, so we kin all get a turn at this stuff," Martha finished.

Resuming my position as teacher, I shooed everyone to their seats. Then I held each book up for examination. Whenever a particular book or magazine caught someone's fancy, it was placed in

142

their outstretched hands for closer scrutiny. Disputes were kept to a minimum with the assurance that there were plenty for all.

I determined that one of the first exercises of the day would be a letter of thanks from each student to Aunt Dolly.

During the eight hectic hours of my school day, my duties as a Temperance Society member were shoved out of my mind. But after I'd swallowed the last plump raisin in my bread pudding at dinner that night, and met Molly Fletcher in the hotel lobby, my wet palms and fluttering insides alerted me to the presence of my old enemy—fear.

Molly waited for me to pull on rubber overshoes, three scarves, a cardigan, cape and overcoat, plus a pair of gloves inside heavy wool mittens. "Miss Bishop," she said hesitantly, "I can't carry a tune in a bucket, and I think I'm losing my voice."

Before my partner changed her mind, I captured her hand between my thick mittens and said, "This morning in my quiet time with God, He gave me a verse. It's from II Timothy 1:7 and it says, 'God has not given us the spirit of fear, but of power and of love and of a sound mind.' I took that as meaning that it's Satan who reduces us to blathering idiots. God expects us to go in His power and love if we're doing this for Him."

With those noble words I flung the door open. We linked arms and, like martyrs on the way to the stake, plowed through the snow sifting from heaven on our way to the National Saloon.

Even with the poor visibility, we couldn't miss it. It exuded bright light through the windows and the swinging half-door. After seeing that door I decided that the happenings inside the saloon apparently insulated its patrons against winter's chill.

Our snow-mantled chairs stood in a splash of light from the door. Mrs. Skillings had already set the stage for her avenging angels. I brushed the snow from the seats. Gingerly we lowered ourselves into the chairs and peeked at each other from beneath our scarves. Subdued voices accompanied by a whiff of tobacco smoke and the tinkling of glasses floated out the door. After what seemed an age, a hoot of laughter punctuated the other muffled sounds from within.

Hesitantly Molly said, "Aren't we supposed to sing?"

Clinging to my morning's promise from God, I whispered back, "Yes. Shall we sing, 'Stand Up For Jesus'? I suppose we *should* stand on that one. Perhaps it'll warm us."

We sounded like a couple of sick canaries on the first stanza and were croaking into the third when Mrs. Skillings materialized from the thickening weather like a snow monster.

"Ladies, ladies," she exclaimed, striking her mittened hands together. "How can we tell the men inside this place of sin about God's ways with such faint voices?"

Swinging her arms in time to the music she bellowed out the words of that rousing hymn. Molly and I could do little else but trill along in her wake.

Oblivious to all but The Cause, Mrs. Skillings waved her arms and stamped her feet in an effort to put some life into her ice maidens. But the wind snatched our words away. I was tempted to join a man who, after one quick glance our way, scuttled through the swinging door into the warmth within.

Finally even Mrs. Skillings succumbed to the elements, tucked her determined chin into her collar and sent us home.

While I thawed out in my fuzzy flannelette nightgown, the Lord and I had a little chat. Emmylou and her doctor bag were out on an errand of mercy and all was quiet. With my fingers wrapped around a steaming cup of tea and my toes toasting upon the open oven door, I confessed that I'd accomplished little for His kingdom, but I praised Him for victory over the fear that all too often tied me in knots. The only apprehension I had now was whether or not my toes would ever regain their sense of feeling.

The next day a curious event snatched all thoughts of temperance obligations from my mind. It involved Ike McAnn. I'd seen very little of him for the past month or so. I'd been so immersed in classroom activities and striving to keep up a daily standard of hygiene that I wasn't left with many spare moments. And when thoughts of Ike had crossed my mind at all, I had imagined him caught up in his courtship of Rose. The twins reported that it had moved into the McGinnis barn. Our weather continued to be so raw that I wasn't surprised.

That evening I'd spoonfed Grandma Espie, as it was one of her poor days and her daughter was busy with the hotel dinner. Tonight there had been no sparkle beneath her hooded lids or witty remarks from those sunken lips. I had appointed myself as the one to see that her food was cut into bite-sized bits and forced between her lips.

Gertie was almost overcome with gratitude.

Actually, I benefited from the act of kindness, too. It provided me with a perfect excuse to avoid my dinner companions who, besides Emmylou, were exclusively male. Deep voices, robust laughter, shaggy brows, hairy faces and blunt, dirt-encrusted fingers snaking bread off platters invariably drove me into my shell. If it hadn't been for Ike's sporadic bursts of laughter, I'd hardly have been aware that our feet were under the same table.

But this evening I looked forward to an enjoyable time of plying my needle and strengthening friendships with congenial companions after dinner. Tonight we initiated Gertie's sewing circle.

In preparation for the event, I'd gone directly from the dinner table to the lobby. In that homey room, I'd tucked myself into a rocker next to the parlor stove. Its round sides pulsated with heat. With my oversized sewing basket on my lap, I'd only had time to arrange my skirt when Ike appeared out of nowhere.

He knelt down next to my chair and, balancing on his toes, favored me with a warm smile. His lips, curving beneath his full red mustache, sent my temperature upward.

His look of amusement told me that he was well aware of my moist palms and scarlet cheeks. "Miss Bishop, I've missed seeing you around. There ain't many ladies that can lay claim to such rosy cheeks and big green eyes. You're a welcome sight on this cold night."

Common sense said, "flatterer," but I said primly, "I've been very busy."

Ike wobbled a bit, then leaned forward. Bay rum tickled my nose as I peeked from beneath my lashes at hair as shiny and black as a crow's wing. He steadied himself by clutching the rocker's arm and suddenly his face was serious.

"Mercy, you are making out all right, aren't you? What I'm saying is, life in this backward town isn't getting you down, is it?"

Finding his solemn side much easier to deal with than his lightheartedness, I confided in him. "I believe it's been good for me. You see, I've never been required to make decisions for myself and accomplish things. Life here in Prospect is forcing me to stand on my own two feet as my Aunt Dolly would say. And yet I'm learning to depend on God more every day. Yes," I continued earnestly, "circumstances the past couple of months have matured me."

"Good," Ike said, his breath brushing my ear. My attention was suddenly drawn to the dining room doorway. Quiet as death Rose stood in a snow-dusted cape. Only her eyes were alive, and they seemed to shoot arrows tipped with hatred.

Protectively, my fingers flew to my lips and Ike's words stumbled to a stop. Following my gaze, he twisted about. Without batting an eyelash, Rose drew him to her like a toy on a string.

Outlined against the big gas lamp hanging over the dining room table, they made a striking silhouette. Possessively she steered him beyond my line of vision toward the door leading to the side porch.

Shifting around in my seat a sense of rejection teased me momentarily. But just then, a beaming Molly Fletcher pulled her chair to my side and engaged me in less melodramatic conversation.

We put our heads together and inspected the

contents of each other's sewing baskets, reminiscing about the origins of various fabric scraps while other ladies filtered into the room. A cozy ladies' sewing circle contrasted with a hostile saloon porch like daylight with darkness.

Gertie, her heart as big as the rest of her, gathered the ladies together with bubbling enthusiasm, gingerbread, and coffee. Informally, we decided to individually piece together four-by-four squares since most ladies had scraps of those dimensions. After we'd each pieced a number, we'd come together again and make a quilt top. The result would be a true crazy quilt. This way everyone would have a part. Perhaps later we'd do a more ambitious pattern, Gertie decided. Maybe a bride's quilt, someone suggested.

Needles flashed and tongues clicked. Subjects were varied, but of mutual interest. No one mentioned the temperance cause and Mrs. Skillings wasn't present to interject the subject. Rose didn't return to the room and while the wind howled down the chimney of the parlor stove, I brushed aside the question of how she and Ike kept from freezing.

Instead, I fastened my attention on the views being exchanged. What was the most successful method of drying venison? Were raspberry leaves effective in curing female complaints? Emmylou's stitches were straggly, but she was very knowledgeable in this discussion. How about salt for chilblains and did anyone have any beeswax to spare? This weather was murder on exposed skin. How did one keep weevils out of cornmeal? And should the Widow Turner be tricking herself out in blue and exchanging confidences with one of the town's confirmed bachelors over the cracker barrel at the store? Everybody knew that Mr. Turner had only met his demise in a railroad construction accident last summer. Mrs. Bristow's confinement was close at hand and let's carry a dish in while she's abed. We flitted from one topic to another and when we parted, our group was united and looking forward to the next meeting of the sewing circle.

Following the dismissal of school the next day, no one loitered. Normally, several of my pupils hung about dragging on mittens, sharing tidbits of information, offering to sweep the floor or clean the blackboard.

But today the sun had turned the snow into a sparkling playground and my students were eager to resume a snowball war begun during noon hour. Books slammed, arms wriggled through coat sleeves, and lunch pails were snatched up while fingers fluttered farewells. Before I could clear my throat, the door slammed on the heels of the last child.

The flurry of departure left a ringing in my ears and fanned the stuffy air. I picked out distinct odors, peculiar to my students, as I perched on the corner of my desk amidst chalk dust dancing in the sun streaming through the windows. The odor of spicy homemade sausage eaten at lunch time lingered, as did the aromatic odor of onion juice smeared on the chests of little bodies encased in winter flannels. Just the smell might ward off coughs and pneumonia, I decided. I noticed, too, how the sun spotlighted the globs of mud beneath James and Orville Bristow's benches.

To my amazement, Rose Hawkins remained. Most days she slipped out sometime during midafternoon. Never had she shared my postclass musings.

149

Today she began advancing toward me as soon as the last child had slammed the schoolroom door.

"Mercy, I believe it is my duty to inform you of something."

My curiosity whetted, I replied, "Yes?"

Stepping up close to me, I was once more aware of her slightly protuberant eyes with the blue vein twitching just above her right temple.

"I believe it's your right to know that Ike McAnn thinks you're a fool" she blurted out. "And his opinion of that Emmylou is the same."

Speechless, I waited.

"Ike's a friendly person so that's why he speaks to you now and then, but don't get the idea he has any regard for you," she sneered, "for he doesn't. He's secretly laughing at you two because he's the one who wrote those letters using Levi Miller's name. And you two were such woodenheads as to answer them, and stupid enough to make the trip all the way out here expecting to land a husband."

She paused, two red spots dotting her fair cheeks, while the blue vein above her temple pulsed with seeming joy.

I shuddered as though one of the icicles from the porch roof had been dropped down the back of my neck.

She continued. "He thinks it's the biggest joke. He intercepted those two letters by telling Mr. Loftus at the store that he was picking up Levi's mail. Then he sent you both answers and waited to see what would happen. The only part that didn't go as planned was you two getting together and not telling Levi. He's had it in for Levi ever since Levi accused him of stealing railroad ties from some cutter."

Regaining my composure I said, "That's very enlightening, Rose. But after meeting Levi we knew he was too fine a person to stoop to such tricks."

She spat out a final warning. "Just you keep your hands off Ike. He's mine and don't you forget it."

Whirling about, she flounced out the door. Shaken in spite of myself, I lost no time in vacating the building. With a limping run, I sped toward home and Emmylou.

Bursting into the cabin, I was annoyed to find Hoss hunched over in one of our chairs. Emmylou stirred a bubbling concoction in a pan on the stove while regarding her patient.

"My vitals is in bad shape," Hoss complained. "And I'm all stove up with rheumatism. I've used horse linament and ain't got wet fer weeks, but I'm chokin' with a misery in my chest."

"Now don't ya fret none," Emmylou soothed as she laid a hand on his slick head and cautiously raised an eyelid. Peering into its depths, she said, "I'm sendin' ya a bottle of garlic juice. Take a swig three times a day and keep rubbin' your linament on. We'll pull ya through yet."

Finally acknowledging my gasping presence, she said, "Howdy, Mercy, ya look ready to bust."

Hoss twisted about, wiped his shirt sleeve across his dripping nose and greeted me. "'Evening, Miss Bishop. Yer friend here is the kindest woman I ever met."

Collecting his medicine bottle and small sack of peppermint for tea, he methodically wrapped several layers of clothing around his ailing body and took his departure.

Almost before Hoss got his aches and pains

through the door, I exploded. "Emmylou, I've just made the most startling discovery."

She raised an eyebrow. "What's that?"

"Rose just told me that Ike wrote those letters using Levi's name."

Surprisingly calm, Emmylou snorted. "I've had that there dude pegged for the one since soon after I met him. Remember that night us three went out on the town? I was right sure then. He's falser than a peg leg. He's always puttin' on he's George's bosom pal, then laughin' up his sleeve at him."

"Well, I hadn't a clue," I admitted. "The whole idea is most disillusioning. But it does fit into place. 'Beware of that man, be he friend or brother, whose hair is one color and mustache another,'" I quoted under my breath.

Emmylou's mouth dropped open. "What's that yer sayin'?"

"It's something Grandma Espie told me the night I met Ike. But more important, what are we going to do now that we know for certain Ike's the culprit?"

"Not a blamed thing. I figure we-uns is the winners and he's the loser. We spoiled his little joke, but good." And she turned to her pan of garlic oil.

I stiffened. "Well, I plan to do something about it. I intend to avoid Ike McAnn like the plague."

Chapter 11

November 24, 1894
Prospect, Montana

Dear Uncle Charlie and Aunt Dolly,

I've been intending to write for some days past, but the press of responsibilities has deterred me.

The box of books and periodicals you shipped by train arrived here at the depot November 4th. There was no damage to the box or the contents and how I wish you could have been present to witness the beaming faces of my pupils as we delved into the treasures that box contained! With books and teaching aids so scarce here in Prospect, they are sincerely an answer to prayer.

I am enclosing messages of gratitude from each pupil. As you will observe, my younger ones (and some of greater age) have not yet mastered the use of a pen and the spelling of the English language, but I believe you will appreciate the "naturalized" copies. James, whom Oak Grove society would label as feeble-minded, is signing his name. Our class is proud of this accomplishment and I refuse to exclude him from our school as suggested by the mayor's wife!

The issues of the St. Nicholas magazine are of special interest to my more advanced students. Their superior stories, poems, nature and science articles have opened up many new doors of knowledge. How I long for a piano to assist our singing from the song books you sent. But alas, the only one in Prospect resides in a saloon!

Lest I tire you with school business, I will close by reporting that my primary class is able to read now and is simply devouring the primers you enclosed. In all honesty, I must confess that I've failed to teach James and his poor, deprived older sister their letters. Progress has been steady with all the other pupils, though, and I'm stretched to the limit when it comes to creating challenging contests for our Friday competitions.

Two requests before I drop this subject: 1. Pray that I will have wisdom in controlling one of my students. (He's taller

than I am and often more clever.) 2. Could
you locate a globe and/or world map for
my geography class?

I refilled my fountain pen from the ink bottle and sorted through the events of the past month to determine which ones wouldn't distress Aunt Dolly unduly. The weather was always a safe topic.

It has snowed so much the past month
that there is six feet of it piled up here in
town. Most people assess this as an
uncommon occurrence, but since the
region has been so recently settled there
are no "old timers" to verify this.

A number of men about town have
formed crews to clear the railroad tracks
as snow slides have a tendency to stop the
train along the way. A train has not made
it through since last week, but it was
announced at the dinner table this
evening that the tracks are nearly cleared.
The deep snows keep men from mining
and wood cutting, also.

I decided not to mention the two bachelors who were suffering from cabin fever according to Emmylou. She'd been called to stitch up a nasty gash after one man hit the other over the head with a frying pan during a feud over a checker game.

Evidently Mr. and Mrs. Bristow were also suffering from the same malady. They refused to speak to one another for two weeks after an argument over whose turn it was to chop the wood. According to the children, who carried the tale to school, they communicated through them. "Alice, tell yer ma to pass the bread" or "Orville, tell yer pa I'm gonna go to the sewin' circle meetin'."

Knowing Aunt Dolly didn't believe life to be perfectly tranquil all the time, I did express my sentiments concerning the thick atmosphere permeating most buildings.

The weather has driven people indoors and the buildings as a whole are of small dimensions, so in short order the climate within reaches such a degree of rankness as to choke the more sensitive. Few doors are open long enough for the foul air to escape and be replaced with fresh. The general opinion is that winter air is detrimental to the health. And that a bath or even a wash-up leads to decline in cold weather. Emmylou, whom I have mentioned earlier as the lady with whom I reside, subscribes wholeheartedly to this view. And since she received medical training at the hand of an Indian, who am I to disagree?

So frequently you find me fleeing into the elements to allow my lungs a deep breath of air unpolluted by an atmosphere heavy with bygone meals, unwashed bodies, slopjars, etc. At these moments I pause to drink in the inspiring view of snow-mantled mountain peaks.

Flexing my cramped fingers, I gingerly tried my unreliable leg, then limped across to the stove and fed its hungry firebox before picking up my narrative.

In an earlier letter I told you of our two ladies' societies, the Women's Christian Temperance Union and the sewing circle. You may be surprised to learn that your retiring niece participates in both. Membership in the first mentioned organization is compulsory for teachers and my support reluctant. Fortunately, attendance at the "saloon sittings" is dwindling, and I expect soon the inclement weather will give the few of us left the courage to disband, albeit fully anticipating Mrs. Skillings' wrath.

The group performed a play, "The Reformed Drunkard's Daughter." I actually dug my heels in, Aunt Dolly, and refused to star in the production. Consequently, I did my duties as the curtain puller (an old bedsheet from the hotel attached to a wire strung across the front of the schoolroom).

No one can convince me that mid-winter boredom didn't have a large part in the house being packed. Whether the audience assimilated the truths portrayed is a matter of conjecture. The "daughter's" staggering death scene did elicit catcalls and boot stompings.

Of the sewing circle, I cannot praise it enough. We are meeting needs: one cheerful quilt pieced, tied and delivered to a poor family of foreigners and another slapped together for a family whose cabin burned to the ground leaving them destitute. (There are no means of fighting fires in our isolated post.) Not only does one enjoy a sense of accomplishment, but visiting freely with other women fills a need in my life and gives me insights into many of the homes of my pupils as their mothers unwittingly reveal snatches of what goes on behind closed doors.

Now I must close this lengthy chronicle, lest it become book length, with a brief account of how I celebrated Thanksgiving miles from the scenes of my childhood.

The Wednesday afternoon before the important day, our students invited parents and friends of the school to witness a production written, produced, and enacted by the class, with a gentle nudge from teacher here and there.

All the songs, recitations and play-acting centered upon praising God. Oh yes, Indians, pilgrims and a turkey did make an appearance. And in spite of one little sprite having "an accident" due to a bad case of nerves and another hiding behind the woodbox, a good number of citizens heard God's Word. And isn't that scriptural? "Out of the mouth of babes and sucklings thou hast perfected praise."

After a morning Thanksgiving service by Reverend Golden, Mrs. McGinnis, the proprietor of the hotel, outdid herself with a lavish feast upon her long table. I'll leave details to your imagination and *draw this missive to a close.*

Affectionately,
Your niece,
Mercy Bishop

Now why, I asked myself, as I creased the linen paper to envelope size, couldn't you bring yourself to tell Aunt Dolly about the most memorable event of Thanksgiving Day? Surely Levi would meet her exacting standards. Wasn't he godly, kind, honest, and patient? Oh yes, all that and more, my heart told me.

But Levi defied a penned description. To my way of thinking, Levi meant blue eyes brimming with kindness, knobby wrists exposed to the weather, shy glances that said, "I think you're nice" and a sheepish grin that cut through the long lines of his face whenever his sense of humor overrode his innate timidity. How could I convey all that to Aunt Dolly—especially knowing she'd share the letter from "her dear niece out in Montana" with all who were interested.

If my locket hadn't disappeared, no doubt Levi and I would have passed Thanksgiving apart. But it *had* vanished while Emmylou and I were attending the sewing circle meeting the Tuesday evening before Thanksgiving.

Earlier, I'd excused myself from the supper table to put some finishing touches on the following day's school program. This task took longer than I'd planned. Rushing back to the cabin to change into a fresh shirtwaist, I'd laid the locket on the board shelf upon which our mirror rested. I was already half an hour late and in my hurry, I'd failed to return the locket to its customary position around my neck.

We discovered its absence when we arrived home after the meeting. I was pulling the pins from the braid coiled on the nape of my neck when I gasped, "Emmylou, my locket's gone. I know I left it here on the shelf. I forgot to put it on after changing. Do you suppose we had a robbery? Oh no," I dismissed that idea with my next breath. "It was gold but not that valuable to anyone but me. I treasured it because it belonged to my mother and had my parents' photographs inside."

Emmylou flew into action, tossing objects right and left, then dropping to her hands and knees to search the floor.

"I know I left it right here," I insisted. "But look, there's a pine cone here now!"

Emmylou heaved to her feet and exclaimed, "It's that thar pack rat. That's their trick every blamed time. Take something shiny and leave ya something outa their nest. Trade off. I'm a-feared your locket's up in the attic in Mr. Rat's nest. Ya recollect I told ya them noises up there were a rat."

Emmylou and I looked overhead at the rough-hewn lumber that functioned as both ceiling and attic floor.

We'd set Levi's trap some weeks ago, only to have the rat's visit coincide with our absence. He'd chewed his way to freedom before we had returned, leaving a large hole in the side of the box. Emmylou'd chopped the mutilated trap into kindling. Then she'd suggested poisoning it with a large dosage of nightshade.

"It's a shame Levi Miller's trap wasn't successful.

160

And poisoning that rat is still offensive to me."

Emmylou shrugged. "Well, suit yourself, honey, but I'll wager we ain't seen the last of that blamed rat."

I considered knocking a board from the ceiling and investigating the dim regions above, but there hadn't been time before Levi came to town.

For the first time in weeks, he'd broken trail and ridden into town from his ranch. A neighbor had offered to feed his stock so Levi took the chance that he could get through the trails in time for the Thanksgiving service, he told me later that day.

Before we could exchange a decent greeting at the church service, Mrs. Skillings dragged him off to confer about the singing and to invite him to share Thanksgiving dinner with them. Dinner would be served at three o'clock sharp provided the twins, who had been left at home, tended to the venison and potatoes and didn't let the fire go out, she had said.

As the meeting began, I nestled into my spot on the bench. On one side I was wedged in by Mrs. McGinnis's ham-sized shoulder and on the other by the brawny biceps of a woodcutter. Mr. Luftus's pudgy back was in front of me. Surrounded by this mass, I felt reduced to a mere speck in a gray felt hat adorned with a full ostrich plume which rippled like a banner.

Thus screened from a view of the pulpit, I peeked around Mr. Loftus's mutton chop sideburns and indulged myself in observing the lanky songleader in his navy blue suit. Oh what luxury to be done with any corrosive little doubts regarding his character! Since first meeting him I had hoped that he was too noble to stoop to deception in obtaining a wife. I'd wanted to believe that if interested he'd be forthright and state his honorable intentions. It seemed I was right. My heart flip-flopped at the thought.

Rationality remained at bay. Emmylou accused me of being moonstruck when, after dropping a fork and spilling my tea during our Thanksgiving feast, I laughed instead of apologizing. But I did pull my thoughts together long enough to realize that additional platters and plates on the table produced a corresponding amount of dirty pots and pans in the kitchen.

So, hopping off the cloud I'd been luxuriating upon, I planted my feet in front of Gertie's work table. Amidst the disorder of the kitchen I rolled up my sleeves, plunged my hands into the hot, sudsy water of the dishpan and wiped a dishcloth across food-encrusted cutlery.

While my hands were employed, my senses soaked up the festive atmosphere of the crowded room. Gertie, in her rocker, rested her overworked feet and occupied an inordinate amount of space, while her three offspring generally impeded progress. Peggy finally threw her hands up in defeat and dumped a stack of plates on the end of a bench, just as Emmylou caught the cat polishing off the gravy. Sally, blithely sketching pictures in the mist of a windowpane, flew to the cat's defense, while Wally and Ben tugged on the turkey's wishbone. Wally staggered back with the big end and bumped into the bench. Both he and the plates crashed to the floor.

We burst into laughter—everyone, that is, but Wally and the cat. The cat leaped for the safety of the cupboard top and Wally propped himself up on one elbow, the picture of bewilderment.

My snickers created a tickle on the end of my nose and I was scratching it with a sudsy hand when the outside door opened and admitted Levi along with a great gust of cold air.

His eyes skimmed the room, stopping when he saw me.

"Mercy Bishop, you've got soapsuds on your freckles," he said solemnly.

While everyone else except Wally and I prolonged their high-spirited laughter, Levi strode over, leaned down and brushed the end of my nose with his mittened finger.

My head spun. By the time I'd regained my composure, Emmylou had appropriated his attention and outlined the plight of my missing locket. Levi offered to delve into the mysteries of our attic the moment the kitchen work was finished.

An hour or so later, the small hole in our ceiling had swallowed all of Levi's long frame, except his toes which dangled from the opening.

Emmylou stood on top of one of my trunks to hand him the lamp. "Now don't ya catch nothin' on fire up there," she admonished.

An incredible amount of dust sifted through the cracks over our heads as he scrambled about in the attic. After only a few moments, his long face, now smudged, appeared through the hole and he cautiously passed the lamp back to Emmylou. She blew it out and vacated the trunk top while he eased his length downward, landing lightly on top of the trunk. Then, reaching back into the hole, he extracted a massive mess.

I held my breath, preparing to dodge a rat, but apparently he'd wisely abandoned his home.

Wrinkling my nose at the foul rat smell clinging to that jumble of grass, sticks and whatall, I marveled in spite of myself at the little creature who'd engineered it.

Setting it on the floor, Levi poked about and soon untangled the chain of my locket which he dropped into my outstretched hand.

"Oh thank you, Levi," I sighed. "I really despaired of ever seeing it again."

"You're most welcome, Mercy, and here's a silver button hook that I expect came from you ladies." Fishing that out he handed it to me, then picking up the nest he walked to the door.

"Let's get this foul-smelling nest out of here."

"Levi, wait," I said. "Don't destroy it. My students will be fascinated. Could we put it in a box and set it next to the porch out of the weather? I'll take it to school Monday so they can see it."

Levi grinned, his teeth pearly white in his dusty face. "Mercy, you do beat all," he approved.

I glowed with pleasure and had spun around to locate the clothesbrush when I caught Emmylou watching us with twinkling brown eyes. Under her breath she said, "You two go together like hugs and kisses."

Blushing and anxious lest Levi hear, I shushed her. "Emmylou, do be quiet, will you!"

But later as I reflected upon the day, I judged it as one of the most satisfying Thanksgivings of my life. And not just because my locket was securely clasped about my neck again, either.

Winter progressed routinely until the Christmas season with the exception of Ike McAnn's disappearance. At the time neither Emmylou nor I assigned any importance to it. Only later did its significance become apparent.

Looking back on the event, we speculated that he might have left Prospect on the first train that came through after the tracks were cleared. Or he might have left on the train that brought Aunt Dolly's Christmas parcel.

Since I'd remained true to my vow to avoid him, I scarcely noticed his presence about town and wouldn't have known he'd left if Rose hadn't approached me in mid-December.

"Mercy," she pleaded, the blue vein twitching frantically, fingers clutching. "Do you have any idea where Ike might be?"

"Why, no," I answered in surprise. "Isn't he about town? I'd think the snow level would keep him from working in the woods."

"Oh, Mercy," she wailed. "Please tell me if he said anything to you."

Irritated with her theatrics, I answered shortly. "I've not exchanged a word with him since you so kindly informed me of his opinion of Emmylou and me. Isn't that what you wanted?"

Satisfied that I did not know his whereabouts, she never questioned me again but she did quiz others. No one, not even Hoss, appeared to have certain knowledge of his movements.

Gertie brushed it off as a common occurrence. "These men all get itchy feet and move on at the drop of a hat."

Emmylou had her theory, too. "That there Rose were gettin' too much the clingin' vine and he jest tore loose. Probably huggin' up to a gal down the tracks somewheres."

As the days grew shorter, the snow grew deeper. Our little town was virtually snowbound. For days the train couldn't make its scheduled stop. Somewhere it stood in the vast wilderness, defeated, its nose wedged into a wall of snow.

But Christmas lies in the heart, I've heard, and the celebration of our Saviour's birth wasn't hampered by our isolation. Rather, it seemed to promote the Christmas spirit. Squabbles were shelved for the season and we pooled our resources and traditions to make Christmas in Prospect a memorable occasion.

One morning the pungent odor of fir boughs greeted us as we opened the schoolroom doors. We discovered a stately evergreen set up in the corner of our classroom.

I cannot say why that one silent specimen of God's creation undermined my orderly schedule and left me with little bodies wiggling and twittering, but I finally accepted defeat and buried my lesson plans beneath a book of Christmas carols.

After this, our school days abounded with sticky paper fabrications, grubby popcorn chains, fervent singing and zealous memorizing of "pieces." Too involved to be mischievous, my little cherubs listened with open-eyed wonder as Reverend Golden strung the Christmas story out for a week. With his droll sense of humor and original gestures, the story of the virgin birth of God's Son came alive.

School closed for the season with an afternoon program and bestowing of gifts. Aunt Dolly had made sixteen handkerchiefs, pink for the girls and blue for the boys. Upon each corner she'd neatly embroidered their names. I'd filled them with hard candy and tied the little bundles with twine, then handed them out at the conclusion of the program. In turn, my basket overflowed with huckleberry jam, homemade pen wipers, potholders, pincushions, and clove apples, while my eyes brimmed at the love they portrayed. My closing remarks were punctuated with sniffles.

After school closed, my Christmas activities centered about the hotel.

Wally and Ben carried the tree to the hotel lobby after Mrs. Skillings ordered its removal from the schoolhouse *cum* church. Trees smacked of paganism, she said.

In this benevolent environment, the humble tree trimmings of my students were overshadowed by bright sugar cookies, glass balls and candles contributed by the boarders and the odd assortment of bachelors who frequented the hotel. Tall as ever, Levi came into town just in time to set the star atop the tree.

After his arrival the festivities took on a special touch for me.

Not once did he denounce any of the practices of Christmas, but in the three days he spent about the hotel, he demonstrated God's love in innumerable ways.

He had a remarkable talent for seeing needs and meeting them. Nothing escaped his notice. To their delight, Wally and Ben's sled came out of retirement after Levi diagnosed its ailments and fixed them.

Woodboxes were never empty. Yuletime goodies cropped up everywhere and Levi had his fingers in their creation. He had stoned the raisins, cracked the nuts, ground the spices, and whipped the cream.

To my way of thinking, the incident that best illustrated his selflessness related to Sally's ball of yarn. With more fervor than skill, she hunched over a frayed ball of yarn the morning before Christmas day, laboriously knitting a potholder for Peggy. By early afternoon the yarn was hopelessly tangled and Sally was reduced to tears. Levi lifted the mass from her lap and spent the rest of the afternoon patiently unraveling the strands. I developed a kink in my neck watching him, but Sally got her second wind and displayed a bumpy, four-inch square of knitting to me after supper.

Aunt Dolly's fears of me becoming hopelessly homesick during the holidays proved unfounded. For the first of my twenty-three Christmases, I experienced first-hand the cozy warmth of a man's arm about my shoulders. This tingling moment occurred while Levi and I were ensconced behind the candlelit Christmas tree. As my glance met his, I saw the flames of the candles mirrored in his eyes. Levi's breath brushed my cheek and I caught my breath in anticipation of my first kiss, when Wally screeched around the tree, causing the candles to flare alarmingly and my heart to sink like a stone.

"Hey you two, Ma wants Levi to lead us in Christmas carols, then we open packages!" he yelled.

Naturally we obeyed, but even Wally's intrusion couldn't dampen my ardor.

Lacking any more really private moments before Levi's responsibilities called him home, I still took every opportunity to be as near him as propriety allowed. As we all gathered on the hotel's back porch to see him off, I took comfort in the fact that his eyes sought me out just before he turned, wrapped and scarved, into the wind. Surely my wits weren't so addled that I couldn't read the message written there. They told me that our parting caused him misery. Not that I wished him misery, but knowing he cared enough to miss me set my heart singing.

I crowded the next few days with mundane tasks in an effort to ease the tickle in my heart, the one I couldn't scratch.

While washing undergarments in the basin at the table one morning, I noticed the date on the calendar which hung on the opposite wall. December 27th. Just one year ago I'd lost my brother Joe in death. How much had changed in the past year, I thought. And me most of all. A year ago I'd had eyes only for myself. I'd rated every event in terms of what it meant to me. This year had taught me much about keeping my eyes on God, "from whence cometh my strength."

Chapter 12

In spite of the below-zero temperature, life in 1895 Prospect reminded me of a simmering cauldron on the verge of boiling. We humans were bubbling, steaming and spewing scalding drops indiscriminately.

If I'd questioned the general population, I'm sure the majority would have agreed to being fed up with ice, snow, raw skin, cold feet and the never-ending task of chopping wood for smoking stoves.

As a member of the community, I was no exception. But as a member of God's family, I felt constrained to exhibit the fruit of the Spirit. However, displaying love, joy, peace, longsuffering, gentleness, goodness, faith, meekness, and temperance was a big order. Before January had advanced into its second week, I'm sorry to say, some of my fruit suffered from bruises.

First of all, Peggy, self-appointed protector of the Paskas, arrived at school with the three little ones in tow.

"Beggin' your pardon, Miss Bishop, but these poor bairns need educatin', do you see?"

"Oh, of course," I agreed, falling on my knees to look into their black eyes. Steadily they returned my look. They were strangers I knew, as I studied their rigid little bodies. They even smelled of spices from distant lands. But Josef, Maria and Erzsabet were still children needing an education. I patted their thick dark hair and introduced them to the class.

Irritable and touchy best described my scholars at this point, but the new little waifs appeared to be a welcome diversion to the group. Fascinated by their meager command of English, the class made a great fuss over teaching them new words.

I was thankful they could not understand more of the language when the Skillings twins strode up to my desk the following morning.

Mary looked down her nose and announced, "Our mother thinks those Paskas ought to be sent home. They're heathen."

"Yup," Martha chimed in, "she says one rotten apple will spoil the whole box."

Slamming my pen on the desk, I said grimly, "Thank you. Now would you two be seated so we can open in prayer? I visited the Bristows last evening and Florence's cough is quite serious. Shall we bow our heads and ask God to heal her?"

I half expected to be confronted by Mrs. Skillings as soon as the twins could reach home and deliver their report. And, indeed, I was, but on a far different matter than the Paska children.

She barged into the schoolroom one evening about a week later. My back was to the door as I stretched to fasten penmanship papers to the line left from the theatrical productions.

I turned as soon as the door slammed. The floorboards quaked under Mrs. Skillings' heavy tread. Without preliminaries she ordered, "Miss Bishop, you sit down. I regret to inform you but I'm the bearer of dreadful tidings."

Stunned, I perched on the corner of my desk.

Clearing her throat she glanced about the room, then dropped her voice to a dramatic stage whisper.

"Miss Bishop, I have learned from the best possible source that Miss Brown is an evil woman. Not only does she carry on under a false name but she murdered—actually murdered—her husband!"

Her odd behavior had caused me to expect the worst. Dizzy with relief, I laughed. "Oh, Mrs. Skillings, you needn't worry about that. I've known about it since we first met. It was a case of self-defense."

For a full moment, her jaw hung limply. Then she snapped her lips shut and shook her fist in my face. Through clenched teeth she said, "Mercy Bishop, you listen to me. You're a foolish young lady. I've questioned your suitability as a teacher of young minds many times but ... but this is too much! I'll give you one more chance. We'll make room for you in our home. Go pack your belongings and flee from that sinful woman."

I leaped to my feet and fired back, "I will *not* move. Emmylou may not know God but she has been more than kind to me and I feel by sharing living quarters with her I can best show her God's ways."

Mrs. Skillings thrust her beaky nose within

inches of mine. "Then you just consider yourself dismissed as the teacher here," she said with fire in her eyes.

Taking a deep breath, I said, "I will not step down as the teacher. You are only one parent and the building belongs to Levi Miller. And I'm sure Levi would agree with me," I finished lamely, hoping my assumption wasn't just wishful thinking.

"Humph!" Mrs. Skillings folded her arms across her chest. "Levi Miller is a God-fearing man and will never condone your wicked behavior. I'm in a position to know. Not only is he an old family friend but the relationship promises to be much closer in the near future."

I drew on my last ounce of courage. "I will remain as the teacher of Prospect School until Levi Miller discharges me," I said stubbornly.

Mrs. Skillings whirled about and stomped out the door.

Before the dust had time to settle, I'd flung on my cape and hurried for the shelter of home.

Once through the door, I clawed my way through damp sheets to discover Emmylou seated at the table. Hands idle, neck rigid, she stared at the far wall. Catching Emmylou in such an unnatural pose startled me. For the moment I forgot the unpleasant scene that had just transpired.

Under my puzzled gaze, the blood rushed back into Emmylou's cheeks. "Mercy, you set yourself down."

For the second time in an hour, I obeyed that command.

Delicacy wasn't one of Emmylou's strong points so she came straight to the point. "That there Rose Hawkins were jest here and I'll be jiggered if she warn't calculatin' on me handin' over a tonic to rid her of that there little baby."

In astonishment, I watched her leap to her feet and slap the table top. In a voice trembling with emotion, Emmylou exclaimed, "Mercy, I tell ya, I were mad enough to spit nails! I shook that there nasty bit of baggage until her teeth rattled. I put a burr in her ear, I'm a-tellin' ya. I said, 'I don't never, *never* use my potions fer killin', only fer healin'.' Then I shoved her through that door afore I did something fierce."

My mind whirled. I struggled to my feet and captured Emmylou's flailing hands.

"Please," I begged, "tell me what's going on. What do you mean Rose and a baby?"

The stony features softened. "Oh ya poor innocent. I 'spects ya weren't mindful of Rose bein' in the family way. I got wise to it when I got a gander of her eyes at the Christmas shindig."

"Her eyes!"

"Yup, I kin always tell by lookin' in their eyes."

"But who . . . what? How? Oh, I don't understand! Who's the father?" I wailed sinking onto the edge of the bed again.

"Honey, that there be as plain as the nose on yer face. Ike McAnn. Ya didn't calculate they were making daisy chains, did ya?"

My eyes widened as I simply stared at Emmylou. My stomach felt as though she had kicked it.

Slipping into her role of doctor, Emmylou dropped to her knees beside me. "Honey, let me give ya a swig of something. I plumb forgot your puny constitution. Don't ya let that Rose plague ya none," she soothed. "She'll always land on her feet.

No call for ya to fret."

Those words, spoken in loving honesty, couldn't have been further from the truth as the significance of Mrs. Skillings' remark about Levi assumed new misery for me.

But I had a week's respite. Mrs. Skillings left me alone, probably taking comfort in the fact that my days as a schoolteacher were numbered in her mind. Somewhat to my surprise, the Skillings children continued to attend school.

The weather was on a warming trend. Tense little bodies were now free to engage in exhausting romps out-of-doors instead of hair pulling and name calling inside.

I'd just snapped the school door shut behind me one Wednesday afternoon in early February when Rose nearly toppled me off the porch.

Breathlessly she apologized. "Sorry, Mercy, but am I glad I caught you! I thought you should be informed concerning my plans."

Puzzled, I watched the red spots come and go on her ivory cheeks. Rose hadn't appeared in the classroom since the Christmas recess so I was at a loss as to why her plans might affect me.

"I feel it is only fair to inform you that I will no longer be assisting you in the schoolroom. I will be marrying soon."

Her large blue eyes which didn't blazon motherhood to me challenged me.

Falling back on courtesy, I merely said, "I wish you well."

This deflated her temporarily but after a moment she stepped forward, forcing my spine into the ivory doorknob. The discomfort of it gouging my back went unnoticed as I absorbed what Rose was saying.

"Bigfoot John rode into town today to tell us that Levi Miller will be coming in this Saturday. We will make our plans with my sister and brother-in-law, then announce our betrothal at Sunday services."

Anyone in the vicinity of Main Street would have never guessed I suffered from a faulty hip by the way I dislodged Rose and sprinted toward home.

Inside, I flopped across the bed and, burrowing beneath the pillow, wept. This was not a ladylike weeping but a wild, abandoned wailing.

After I'd spent myself in sorrow, I sat upright, flung off my jacket and examined the cold, ugly facts. Rose's motives for becoming Mrs. Levi Miller were not pure ones. She did not love him. Rose only meant to use Levi's name to cover her shame.

On the other hand, if love meant desiring the best for the loved one, then I was the one who loved Levi. If I'd mistaken his intentions and his affections pointed elsewhere, I would mournfully let go. But Rose hadn't even shown any interest in Christ and surely Levi wouldn't consent to marry a non-Christian?

In the middle of my mental anguish, Emmylou arrived home. Her perceptive eyes seemed to sense my grief. She plopped her musty presence on the bed and the springs groaned.

"Honey, what ails ya?"

"Oh, Emmylou," I blubbered, "Rose just told me that she and Levi plan to marry."

To my surprise, Emmylou threw her head back and laughed. "Oh, Mercy, that man's got more smarts than to git hitched up with that there slyboots."

"Do you really think so, Emmylou? She told me they mean to announce their betrothal at Sunday services. It seems Bigfoot John brought the

177

message that Levi plans to come to town on Saturday. And Mrs. Skillings will be throwing her weight for the match, I know. Do you think she knows about Rose's condition?"

Emmylou studied a cracked fingernail, then shifted her gaze to me. Concern shown in her brown eyes. "That there woman may have her eyes fixed on heaven, but she ain't likely to have missed that. She knows." Emmylou thought a moment. "And if she do know, she shore would connive to git Levi to marry up with that Rose.

"And I've been a-ponderin'. You know Levi's got a heart as soft as butter in July and Rose's got more tricks up her sleeve than a magician. Jest supposin' Levi's pitying ways let Rose hog tie him?"

"Oh, Emmylou, say that won't happen," I pleaded.

"Ya truly loves that man, don't ya?"

"Yes," I answered simply.

"Well," said Emmylou as she hopped off the bed, "ya let me do a spell of brainwork. I'm gonna cook up a pot of starch for them there shirt collars. Don't ya fret none. Where there's a will, there's a way."

I didn't answer Emmylou. Instead, I rolled over on the bed so my back was to the room. My eyes focused on a knot in the wall as I poured my heart out in silent anguish to God. "Oh Lord, you know I want your will for my life. That's the only way I've ever been happy. But you let me come out here to Montana when I assumed I would be marrying Levi. He has turned out to be the upright Christian gentleman I thought, and I love him. If it is in your will for me to marry him, I just want to let you know that's what I want, too. Show me your way and lead me in your paths, above all else. Thank you, Father, for listening and for the answers I know will come," I finished in my heart.

The cornstarch bubbles had just begun to pop when Emmylou set it aside and called me to join her at the table.

When I had, she said, "Mercy, I've hit on a plan. Now," she cautioned, "don't ya go hornin' in 'til I've given it to ya straight. Tomorrow morning, bright and early, we'll put ya on George Hoofnagle's old mare and send ya up to Bear Canyon to Levi's."

I jumped to my feet, horrified. "Emmylou, wait! I can't! You don't understand. I completely fall apart around horses and I could never ride one," I said emphatically.

Emmylou shoved me back into the chair. "Now ya listen here, Mercy Bishop," she told me sternly. "Ya kin do it. Ain't ya the one that's on first names with God? Jest tell Him to git on behind and hold ya on. That old mare's so gentle it'll be like settin' in a rockin' chair."

"Emmylou, you don't understand about God. As one of His children, His Spirit lives inside me. I don't have to pray and ask Him to be beside me, and in the book of Hebrews, God tells us He'll never leave us or forsake us."

Emmylou's face lit up. "Well, I'll be blamed if that ain't even better. Ya won't need to be scared none at all with God right in ya. Ya know, Mercy, I'm ponderin' on learnin' about what the Bible says. You really are a lady, more'n jest the way you was raised. I figure it has to do with that God of your'n. Reckon I'll deck myself out in that fancy dress ya made me and take George up on his invite to Sunday services."

I knew my Christian witness was at stake, so what could I say after that but, "Emmylou, riding a horse will still be a terrifying experience but I can't doubt God after what He's seen me through this past year. I guess I got my eyes off God for a moment and back on myself and my problems."

Silence reigned for a moment. "But once I'm at Levi's, what do I do then?"

"Honey, when ya clap eyes on that there dude, jest spill the beans. Tell him how ya feel 'bout him. After that, if I'm not missin' my guess, ya won't be needin' no help from yer old friend Emmylou."

We were silent a moment while I considered Emmylou's plan. It meant completely ignoring Miss Prince's "Etiquette For Young Ladies." A cardinal rule was that a young lady never calls upon a gentleman.

Another obstacle came to mind. "What about my classroom? If I don't arrive for class, Mrs. Skillings won't rest until she learns of my whereabouts."

"Don't let that bother ya none. I'll play teacher and I'll do my blamdest to cover your tracks. We'll git ya headed out early and I'll jest leg it over to the school. I ain't much fer readin' and writin', so's tomorrow they's going to git lessons in herbs, cures, potions, and such."

"I'll do it," I decided, "but only because I'll not draw an easy breath until I've spoken to Levi."

"Well, I'll skedaddle over to see George and git the loan of old Tilly," Emmylou said cheerfully. "Ya wait and see, everything'll turn out topside."

I longed to share her optimism. Would God really bless such a crazy scheme?

*   *   *

180

I spent a restless night, dominated by nightmares . . . a mare named Tilly who bit me, trampled me and generally oppressed me in my sleep. When I woke up at the crack of dawn, I looked and felt like an empty gunnysack.

Under a faded print wash dress, my legs were encased in an old pair of George's trousers. I'd been pinned into this article of clothing since my promoters, Emmylou and George, had determined I'd encounter fewer problems riding astride than sidesaddle. Farewell forever to Miss Prince of the Female Academy! I shuddered.

Emmylou steered me toward the barn behind George's cabin. "Ya walk like you've got a log between your legs."

"It feels that way, but even straddling a log I'm apt to change my mind and run away, so don't let me go," I warned.

"I ain't gonna give ya the chance," Emmylou assured me. "Lookee, there's George with Tilly now."

In the dim light I could barely see George standing beside a horse that looked about as sorry as its owner. I took comfort from the fact that it had long passed the wild-eyed, snorting, stamping stage that invariably sent me into a panic. This beast merely sagged.

Nevertheless, a long shudder coursed through me.

"What's the odds," George greeted us gloomily. "Looks like we're in for rain."

"Oh no," Emmylou contradicted. "It's gonna be a purty day. Come on Mercy, quit diggin' your heels in. Come over here and make friends with Tilly."

She placed my hand on Tilly's coarse mane.

Butterflies danced in my stomach as that odor peculiar to horses assailed my nostrils. But before Tilly or I could protest, Emmylou and George each latched onto an elbow and flung me through the air, causing me to land with a plop in the saddle. There I teetered until I seized the saddle horn.

I stiffened and my legs stuck out at the sides like posts. "It's miles to the ground," I protested weakly.

"Nah, old Tilly's only about fifteen hands high, almost a pony," George argued, mopping the end of his nose with his shirt cuff.

He led the horse around the barn to the head of the trail while I hung on for dear life. Then, he placed the reins in my knotted hands and gave me a two minute lesson on steering the beast I straddled.

"Now just stay on the trail. It follows the mountain around and when you get to a turn-off about two and a half miles up, you take the left fork. You'll be able to look down into Bear Canyon and see Levi's place from there. Just follow the left fork and it'll take you to his front gate."

With those scant directions, he slapped Tilly on the flank and we were off!

"Jest relax, honey," Emmylou hollered, as Tilly fell into a steady gait.

Afraid to shift positions, I couldn't look back so I settled in for the duration. I couldn't move physically but my mind ran rampant. Two concerns tormented me. First, what did I do if Tilly decided to deposit me in the middle of the trail; and second, were the bears out of hibernation?

Slowly and steadily, Tilly took me toward Levi. Perhaps Mrs. Skillings was right, I thought with dismay. Levi might reject me when he learned of Emmylou's past. And what would he think of a lady who was bold enough to approach him about such a delicate subject as Rose's condition? But there was no turning back.

Contrary to George's predictions, the sun put in an appearance and its warmth caused moisture to accumulate beneath my wool cape and George's rough trousers. I itched in the most unladylike places. *You must endure*, I told myself grimly, *for any twitching might unseat you.*

As Emmylou had said, Tilly's gait could be compared to a rocking chair. But from the pain developing in my backside, I'd say the rockers had a clog beneath them.

Too tense to appreciate any passing scenery, I focused upon my hands gripping the saddle horn and on balancing my bottom. My legs grew numb and a pain jabbed my hip.

Through my misery I perceived that Tilly's rhythm had slacked off a bit. Peeking from under my lashes, I noticed a fork in the trail and a path plunging downard to the left. Carefully turning my head, I looked in that direction. About a mile away, down in a valley, I saw several buildings grouped together in the middle of a meadow.

I tugged on the left rein and, thankfully, Tilly obliged. My short lesson on horsemanship hadn't included points on retaining one's balance when the horse's head was several feet lower than its tail, however! As Tilly headed downward, I flopped across the saddle horn and clutched tightly at her neck hairs. She interpreted this as an indication that I wanted her to go faster. She picked up speed as we bounced down the mountain and out into the flat. The wind whistled past my ears and I heard the sound of barking dogs. Prying one of my closed eyes open, I noticed several large, gangly dogs yapping at Tilly's heels. I closed my eyes again, sure that death was imminent.

Then, quite unexpectedly, Tilly halted and I sailed from the saddle into the security of Levi's arms. Terrified I clutched at his neck and buried my face in his shirt front. It smelled of freshly laundered wool.

Levi's voice asked anxiously, "Mercy, what's wrong? Are you all right?"

As he set me on the ground, I noticed the top of my head just reached his heart. Its steady beat was most reassuring.

"Mercy, what's the matter?" Levi repeated. His long fingers shook my limp frame slightly. Evidently he feared he had a swooning lady on his hands and, somehow, I didn't mind the idea.

But before I received a splash of water in my face or perhaps worse, I decided I'd better answer. Without looking up, I stammered, "Levi, I...I... trust you'll forgive the impropriety, but I just had to see you before Rose did."

Planting my hands on his shirt front, I pushed back until I could look up into his eyes. They were filled with questions.

"Oh Levi, Rose means to trick you into marrying her to cover the shame of bearing a child out of wedlock. And—and she doesn't love you, as I do."

Levi removed a comforting arm from about my middle to tug on an ear. "What's all this?" he asked incredulously.

I took a deep gulp and began. "Well, Rose was real

friendly with Ike McAnn the past few months and . . . and . . . she asked Emmylou for some medicine and it seems there's to be a child . . . . Meanwhile Ike disappeared from town back in November and so Rose needs a husband and . . . and, she told me that you two were making arrangements to announce your betrothal this Sunday and oh, Levi, Emmylou says you have better sense, but I just had to hear it from your lips. Please tell . . . ."

The tiniest glint of laughter was starting to lighten the concern in Levi's blue eyes when my babbling was cut short by Levi's dogs. They'd been napping about our feet but now leaped up, vigorously announcing the presence of another morning caller.

Levi's arms tightened around me as we turned to see a horse speeding down the trail. Properly attired in a gray riding habit, Mrs. Skillings perched sidesaddle atop a long-legged bay mare.

Expertly she brought her horse to a halt, inches from my nose. With Levi's arm encircling my waist, I stood my ground without flinching until she shot from the saddle and shook her fist in my face.

"Miss Bishop, I demand an explanation of your unseemly behavior. You leave your position of responsibility in the hands of a murderess to free yourself to call upon a gentleman unchaperoned. And then, as much as I'd like to deny it, I catch you in his embrace like a brazen hussy."

Her face was a mottled red and her eyes, behind her glass lenses, popped out every bit as much as her sister's. Instinctively, I moved closer to Levi, as he jerked to attention.

"Mrs. Skillings, we are friends of long standing,

but that does not give you license to speak to my betrothed in such a rude manner. I insist upon an apology."

"Your—your—what?" she sputtered, hopping about like she had a bee under her skirts.

Levi gently turned me within the circle of his arms until he was facing me. Looking down at me from his great height he said softly, "Mercy, would you do me the honor of becoming my wife?"

I looked up into his clear blue eyes and read a message of love there. "Oh, Levi, I'd be so happy to be your wife," I told him lovingly.

Reveling in an entirely new sensation, we forgot our audience until she cleared her throat. "Well, I never! This is highly irregular. I've never considered you a suitable teacher, Mercy Bishop, and this just proves how right I was."

Reluctantly we turned.

"Oh, you needn't concern yourself," Levi said, his hand slipping down to hold mine. "I'll be taking care of Mercy here on our ranch. You'll have to find yourself another teacher."

The sun which had taken refuge behind a cloud emerged to cast its benediction on Levi's pronouncement.

Turning around I shed my cape and joyfully surveyed my new home. Levi and I stood in front of a white gate set into a fence that enclosed a cluster of tidy buildings. The walk beyond the gate led to a porch which ran the length of a sizable house. I just knew a red checkered tablecloth would add to its snug interior.

For once at a loss for words, Mrs. Skillings fell back on her wounded authority and ordered, "Mercy, you get on your horse right now. We're going back to town. Perhaps we can save a part of your good name."

Levi's face crinkled into a smile. "Don't worry overmuch about the Bishop part of her name," he teased, looking at me with a loving light in his eyes. "That's going to be changed to Miller before long."

"Levi Miller this is not a time for levity. This foolish young lady has bewitched you. I just hope you won't be sorry about this hasty decision," Mrs. Skillings said as she whirled about and mounted her horse.

Unfortunately we knew part of what she said was right. We'd stretched the limits of propriety as far as we could for today. Levi picked me up easily and seated me tenderly on Tilly. Then he folded my hands about her reins. "Mercy, I'll be in town the day after tomorrow. We'll make our plans then," he promised softly.

A bubble of happiness choked off any speech, but I saw my love mirrored in Levi's eyes as he looked up at me.

Of the second horseback ride of my life, I recall practically nothing. I do remember that even in my state of euphoria, pity for Mrs. Skillings stabbed me a time or two. The rigid spine atop the horse that Tilly followed was a bit more limp than I was accustomed to seeing it.

But by the time we came in sight of George's weatherworn barn with the tired snow piled against its shady side, she'd snapped back to normal and appeared ready to forgive my transgressions.

"Good day, Miss Bishop," she said, twisting easily in the saddle. "I believe I'll ride over to Thomas Henderson's and give him an invitation to supper.

Those bachelors do appreciate a meal with a family."

I nodded my head, afraid to slacken my grip on the saddle horn, and decided I needn't worry about Rose. With Mrs. Skillings on the case, she'd be entering the state of matrimony before Levi and I finalized our plans.

Mrs. Skillings rode off.

Tilly plodded up to George's barn door and quit. With a heavy sigh, all of her big bones slouched and suddenly the ground appeared much closer.

But before I could courageously slide from her back, Mary—or it might have been Martha—sailed past red-faced and puffing with Wally hard on her heels.

"Now, what's that about?" I asked myself as my feet hit solid ground.

Before my curiosity could be satisfied, Emmylou appeared.

"Mercy Bishop! Ya don't need to say a word," she exclaimed. "Them big old green eyes are justa dancing."

"Oh Emmylou," I bubbled. "You were right. As soon as I sailed into his arms, I couldn't help but tell him that I loved him."

"Ya sailed into his arms? Well I'll be a monkey's uncle!"

"Emmylou, I didn't plan to, honest, but Tilly stopped so quickly. And then Mrs. Skillings caught me there and became most accusing, but Levi stood his ground and told her we were betrothed. And he *isn't* going to marry Rose Hawkins, so how would you like to be the honor attendant at our wedding?"

"Me!" she shrieked. "I always recollected that

brides asked their best friends to stand up with 'em."

"They do," I agreed, "and you show me a better friend."

"Oh, Mercy, I'm a-gonna blubber over fer sure," she said as her eyes sparkled with tears. "And after I ruint our idea to head that there Mrs. Skillings off. She showed up at the school and weren't about to let up until I spilled the beans about where you'd went. She said she'd get the sheriff onto me if I didn't 'fess up. But jest like ya told me, God was a-takin' care of ya."

Ruthie, Elizabeth and Sally skipped into view, their fingers intertwined and their faces screwed into puzzled lines.

"Where have you been?" Ruthie demanded of me.

"The boys are being ornery," Sally said while twisting the end of a braid.

Responsibility settled upon my shoulders once again. "Why yes, Emmylou, why are the children running loose?"

Emmylou sighed. "I'll be blamed, Mercy, but I gotta hand it to ya. How ya keep them little urchins corralled is more than I can savvy. After about an hour, I jest opened the door and turned 'em out."

Ruthie said admiringly, "She shore put Wally in his place, though."

"Well, I had to do somethin' with that scamp," she said defensively. "He was makin' a ruckus you wouldn't a-believed. So's I jest twisted his ear until he hollered 'uncle.' Ya orta try it."

My hand flew to my mouth. "Oh goodness, I'd never be able to do that!" I cried. "But I'd better hurry to the school and round up my students before they scatter beyond the sound of the bell."

Smiling down at my little girls, I caught a glimpse of my attire and squealed. "Emmylou! Just look at me!"

Clapping my hands to my head, I found hair dangling over my ears and drifting down the neck of my faded wash dress, now liberally trimmed with horse hairs. And most disgusting of all, George's trousers had fallen into bulky folds about my ankles.

"Oh, Emmylou," I wailed. "What a fright I look! How could Levi have looked at me with love brimming from his eyes and then propose to such a wreck? I completely forgot my appearance."

"I'll wager his mind weren't on it neither. And honey, ya got a button missin' on yer dress."

"I do?" I gulped as I dropped my gaze. Sure enough, an empty buttonhole gaped halfway down the bodice of my dress.

"Now, don't let that give ya the fidgets," Emmylou advised. "Didn't ya tell me that God don't look at the outside, but on the innards?"

"Yes," I said, calming down as I recalled my words of several months past. "And to think I've gotten my eyes on myself again. How could I, after God protected me and gave me a safe ride to Levi. And—oh, Emmylou, He gave me Levi, too!"

I looked into Emmylou's eyes. They were brimming with an infectious glee that swept me into its wake. I hugged myself with joy while Tilly swished her tail and swung her head, snorting through blubbery lips.